Beyond The [Himple' Advent

To Elsie Rose

It was great to Meet you!

/Astubbs.

Mark A. Stubbs

Printed in the United Kingdom

First Printing, 2021

Published with SEO ProHub UK

Table of Contents

Dedication

To all my family, especially my daughters, Poppy and Amy. You are my everything

Acknowledgement

Firstly and most importantly, I need to thank Sarah Jane, my wife, who sent out the first manuscript to publishers, whose replies were overwhelming. She was my editor in chief, proof reader, grammar teacher and taskmaster. Without her, Himple would never have happened.

There are so many people to thank who have let me twitter on about dwarves, editors and confusing grammar. Thank you for not telling me to shut up!

Special mentions go to my daughters, Poppy and Amy, who watched Himple's story grow and, by their reactions, told me what was good and what needed a rewrite.

To the SEO Pro Hub team for making it happen - Kevin, Walter, and Isaac, thank you for believing in me.

To Stephen Martin, Juliet Perkins, Victoria and Paul Stubbs and the whole of Year 6 21/22 at St Peter's Primary School in Bromyard, for vital help.

Support comes in many ways, so it's important to mention my parents Andy and Gill Stubbs, and my in-laws, Kevin and Angela Mylotte, for all their help.

Lastly, to a writer that has truly captured my family's imagination and has been an inspiration to me, especially with his kind email of support, to Kieran Larwood and the amazing Five Realms Books. May we all aspire to be bards in our own way.

Thanks All!

About The Author

Mark A. Stubbs was brought up in rural Herefordshire, in the small village of Bishops Frome. He had a great childhood with brother Paul, enjoying the freedom of the countryside. He was never far away from a drawing pad and getting lost in his own imagination. Mark loved school and was the Head Boy of the Queen Elizabeth High School in the nearby town Bromyard, where he now lives. Mark is now a managing director of a packaging company. In his spare time, he is a volunteer Guide, Brownie and Rainbow helper "Artist Owl" and has become a favourite with the girls. Mark played Table Tennis for many, many years, winning many local titles and representing his county Herefordshire until he was hit down with AVN and other mobility limiting conditions. Although now disabled, Mark still loves to experience the countryside with his wife, Sarah-Jane, and daughters, Poppy and Amy, and naughty labradoodle, Barkley.

Introduction

Most people think that fairy-tale creatures were created to entertain and scare children. Have you ever thought it is quite a coincidence that the exact same characters appear in stories all around the world? Gnomes, fairies, dragons and even dwarfs appear in stories from every corner of the world going back to ancient times. All the same creatures found in all these ancient cultures is not a coincidence.

Now before I can tell this tale, I must explain how things work, as there is a lot more to these tales than meets the eye. The children of today are not so easily hoodwinked and fooled into believing things blindly. Let's bring science into the equation now. You have probably heard the phrase "of another realm." Ever given it a serious thought? Some far-off mystical place with castles and a princess or two? What if I said alternate reality or space-time events? Sounds more interesting? These are the same thing. One makes you think princesses and the other dark and scary sci-fi stuff. Occasionally there is a breakdown, a split in the fabric of time and reality between our world and other dimensions, including the place where the characters from our folktales and traditions live.

The splits were more open and accessible in the past. You may know a few of them, Stonehenge, for example, and the Taulas Stones in Menorca. Our ancestors, in times long ago, knew about this, and creatures like hungry dragons, for example, could pop through for a snack a bit like visiting the local shop. The snack could be some villagers or princess or two. Ever wondered what Stonehenge was for? Well, now you know.

The gates of Beyond are like Stonehenge. They are doors to our world and other realms. This is the reason the creatures, "mystical fairy tale creatures", from Beyond appear around our world as they could visit multiple locations from the gateway. Did I mention the other realm was called Beyond? Good, so is this all beginning to make sense? Beyond is the world of dwarfs, dragons and other mythical creatures. Maybe by the time we are finished, you can explain it to an adult, but I do not fancy your chances. Adults are so very much stuck in the confines of their own beliefs. The inhabitants of Beyond would often visit our world in the past. I am sure you have heard many tales of dragons and mermaids. Indeed, it is said that wars and natural disasters have destroyed all, but a few of the gateways and those left are so occupied by humans, visiting creatures from Beyond now stay away. Well, not all of them...

Good, as you know, most of what goes on here in our realm so let me fill you in about the other side. Beyond is another version of our earth living at the same time as us in another reality, so you have the lands known to us as Europe mainly occupied by gnomes and fairies, the odd leprechaun, and giants in Ireland, but a lot of them would play a silly game of balancing and hopping from stone to stone on the Giants Causeway as I would call it. To be more exact, it is the Giants Gateway, another like Stonehenge. Not being very bright, the working of the gateway annoyed the giants so much they took to chucking the stones into the sea. They often threw them so far, and they ended up in North America!

The Gateways

Chapter One: Life Was Quiet In Beyond

Dragons kept themselves to themselves, and the ongoing conflict between mermaids and banshees had settled down recently. There was a time when mountain trolls and dwarfs went to war over who owned the mountains, and gryphons and dragons fought for the skies. So, all in all, things were good.

There was little need for transport to the other realms, although an occasional drunken gnome had been known to fall through, and of course, leprechauns often would pop through in the search for a pot of gold.

Himple was not keen on normal academic life. Staying under the radar was his main aim in the day. That was not to say he didn't want to rebel; it was all he thought about some days. He would love to pick a fight with his axe master. Maybe not an actual fight, as axe masters are very good at fighting. Maybe he could pick a fight with Master Drippings, his Mountain Arts master. He was so old he would put up much of a fight. He only got excited enough to lift his axe if there was a rock formation in need of investigation. `

Himple walked to the Dwarf Academy every school day. The academy was a couple of miles from the town where he lived. He scanned the hedges for wildlife and flowers, checking out changes from the day before. He liked to look out over the lake at the birds. The academy was near the

Realm Gateways. This was unusual. Realm Gateways and inquisitive young minds were not generally a good combination. This academy had been entrusted with the education and teachings of Realm Gateways. It was one of the oldest academies in the land. Himple's day was made up of the Final Year Foundational Dwarf Skills. These were lessons in Axe Handling. They included how to maintain and use your axe in a variety of situations, what types of axes to use and what materials they were made up of. Mountain Knowledge, both digging and stone recognition, made up a large part of the graduation exams and would be, for most graduating dwarfs, the most likely type of employment in their futures. Brewing - beer and mead making and finally the Art of Warfare, both historical and modern techniques, completed the foundation studies. It had to be said Himple excelled at none of these and barely enjoyed them. The only one that could have interested him was stone recognition, but as Master Drippings spent at least half the lesson asleep, he had never built up any interest in it either.

There were, however, a few specialist lessons they were forced to attend every week. Not main core subjects but part of dwarf life, you may say. These subjects Himple really enjoyed. They were: Knowledge of the Realm Gateways. This was Himple's real passion - exotic places with unusual animals, plants and strange climates. Beard Trimming – Himple wasn't sure why he enjoyed this but keeping his beard trimmed gave him a deep amount of satisfaction. Himple did like things "just so." His absolute favourite was Realm Creatures. Himple loved animals of all kinds; the thought of travelling through the gateway to destinations where exotic creatures lived was his aim in life. He had an almost encyclopaedic knowledge of animals and their habitat, foods they eat and the special abilities that mystical creatures often had.

Today was Monday, and Realm Creatures being his final lesson of the day, gave Himple something to look forward to...He needed it to get through the earlier lessons of the day.

"Himple, if you continue to hold that axe like you are going to pee out of it, you will never make a mark in that tree!!!!" shouted Master Grimtrunk. Master Grimtrunk was certainly not Himple's favourite teacher. He favoured those dwarfs that had more muscle than brain. Himple was concerned that unless the end of year exams "the D.R.A.G.'s" were about anything other than hitting things hard with an axe, they were all in a lot of trouble. Himple was practising synchronised tree felling with the only real friend he had, Barnaby Grabbage, a rather overweight dwarf who it had to be said was two or three years (possibly more, but Himple didn't like to ask) over the normal 10 years young dwarfs spent at the academy. The exercise involved taking turns to hit the same spot on the tree with the target of chopping it down. Himple was reasonably happy with the way it was going when Grimtrunk interrupted them, "Grabbage, you have been taking my class for 20 years, and my granny would have more chance of felling that tree!!!"

Having seen Grimtrunk's granny at the last open day competing in the over 200-year-old stone carrying contest, he was indeed correct, but it was very unkind to say so. Grimtrunk often picked on Himple and Barnaby, despite them being one of the better groups in the class. Himple's brain and Barnaby's strength made for a good combination. Despite this, Grimtrunk hated them more than he hated all students and was not shy at making his feelings known.

Himple was glad the day was over, and he very much enjoyed the Realm Creatures lesson but was not looking forward to taking home his final school report of the year. His father was home early from the mine. He had fed and watered the donkeys and animals he looked after, cleaned their stables, and was home sitting at the kitchen table with a beer in hand, waiting for his only son's return. Himple's mother did what dwarf women did, tended their range cooking and baking. Himple's mum was a little overprotective of him.

"Let me check your hand for blisters," Himple's mum shouted as he opened the door, "That idiot axe master is a brute!" "Leave the young dwarf alone, Gwen!" His dad interrupting the hand inspection, went on, "How was school today, my boy? Lots of fascinating facts for me, I hope!" "You know Griffins lay no more than 4 eggs at a time? Well, there was one in the Mountains of Griff last month that laid 9!" Himple's face came alive as he relayed the story to his father.

"I got my report today. I will leave it on the side, and I will go and feed the girls", said Himple, and he beat a hasty retreat to the backyard. Horace Gwim sat quietly and read the report.

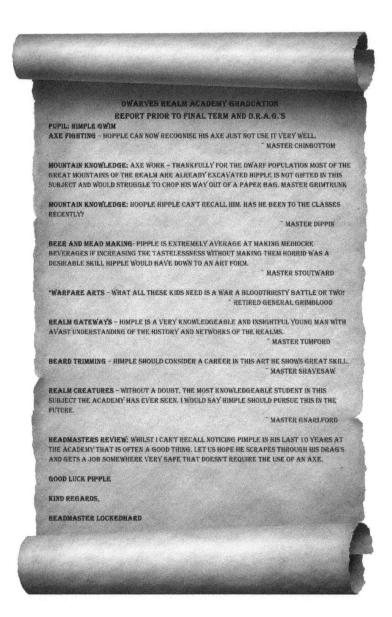

DWARVES REALM ACADEMY GRADUATION
REPORT PRIOR TO FINAL TERM AND D.R.A.G.'S

PUPIL: HIMPLE GWIM

AXE FIGHTING – HOPPLE CAN NOW RECOGNISE HIS AXE JUST NOT USE IT VERY WELL.
¯ MASTER CHINBOTTOM

MOUNTAIN KNOWLEDGE: AXE WORK – THANKFULLY FOR THE DWARF POPULATION MOST OF THE GREAT MOUNTAINS OF THE REALM ARE ALREADY EXCAVATED HIPPLE IS NOT GIFTED IN THIS SUBJECT AND WOULD STRUGGLE TO CHOP HIS WAY OUT OF A PAPER BAG. MASTER GRIMTRUNK

MOUNTAIN KNOWLEDGE: HOOPLE HIPPLE CAN'T RECALL HIM. HAS HE BEEN TO THE CLASSES RECENTLY?
¯ MASTER DIPPIN

BEER AND MEAD MAKING- PIPPLE IS EXTREMELY AVERAGE AT MAKING MEDIOCRE BEVERAGES IF INCREASING THE TASTELESSNESS WITHOUT MAKING THEM HORRID WAS A DESIRABLE SKILL HIPPLE WOULD HAVE DOWN TO AN ART FORM.
¯ MASTER STOUTWARD

*WARFARE ARTS – WHAT ALL THESE KIDS NEED IS A WAR A BLOODTHIRSTY BATTLE OR TWO!
¯ RETIRED GENERAL GRIMBLOOD

REALM GATEWAYS – HIMPLE IS A VERY KNOWLEDGEABLE AND INSIGHTFUL YOUNG MAN WITH A VAST UNDERSTANDING OF THE HISTORY AND NETWORKS OF THE REALMS.
¯ MASTER TUMFORD

BEARD TRIMMING – HIMPLE SHOULD CONSIDER A CAREER IN THIS ART HE SHOWS GREAT SKILL.
¯ MASTER SHAVESAW

REALM CREATURES – WITHOUT A DOUBT, THE MOST KNOWLEDGEABLE STUDENT IN THIS SUBJECT THE ACADEMY HAS EVER SEEN. I WOULD SAY HIMPLE SHOULD PURSUE THIS IN THE FUTURE.
¯ MASTER GNARLFORD

HEADMASTERS REVIEW: WHILST I CAN'T RECALL NOTICING PIMPLE IN HIS LAST 10 YEARS AT THE ACADEMY THAT IS OFTEN A GOOD THING. LET US HOPE HE SCRAPES THROUGH HIS DRAG'S AND GETS A JOB SOMEWHERE VERY SAFE THAT DOESN'T REQUIRE THE USE OF AN AXE.

GOOD LUCK PIPPLE

KIND REGARDS,

HEADMASTER LOCKEDHARD

* (This has been put on every one of his pupils' reports since he left the army 96 years ago)

9

Himple

Chapter Two: The Girls

Pets are an experience most of us have had over the years in the form of goldfish, maybe a gerbil, or a cat, or dog. Dwarfs were not big pet owners, but Himple and his father loved animals. In particular, they had a love for the exotic. bugganes are, of course, rather unusual, even in Himple's realm. Basically, a bear crossed with a mole, they had three beautiful ladies, Panda type bugganes with big digging claws and silky smooth black and white fur, poor eyesight but well trained for a ferocious creature. To Himple's knowledge, they were the only bugganes kept for pets anywhere. They were rarely kept at all, maybe in large mines for digging in areas even dwarfs dared not go. Then in these cases, they were heavily chained and led to a very sad existence.

Himple poured them fresh water and threw them some melons. He loved to sit in their enclosure and stroke them. They were always pleased to see him. One of them was particularly special. Himple had named her Mabel, and she loved Himple. She stood at least twice his height with silky black fur apart from a white patch over her eye. These were wild animals who were feared in the wild. The only reason they had not been hunted to extinction was their ability to dig. They made large caves and tunnels in the wild and saved lots of work for the dwarfs. To Himple's knowledge, his father was the recognised expert on bugganes, but not even his father would venture too close to them, let alone sit and cuddle Mabel. That was something only Himple could do.

His father wandered out, leaning against the fence, tugging on his beard. He did this when he was struggling with the right words. He looked across at his son, who was sitting next to Mabel on the floor like a baby in a big fury armchair. "You know you could pass everything if you just embraced the subjects you don't like as much as you do the ones you like. Most of the blithering idiot masters couldn't even remember your name!" Himple knew his dad was right. If only the subjects and teachers made him want to learn more. "I don't mind hard work, dad; I just don't think how hard you can hit a rock should be the reason you can pass exams and leave school." Himple put his head in his hands as he spoke. "Grimtrunk wants me to fail. He always had!"

"Well, I may have something to do with that. I think I ought to explain." Himple's dad tugged some more on his beard and lit his pipe. "Grimtrunk and I go way back. Too far. I know too much, I guess. We were friends, you see, classmates. He was the strongest and fastest and I was the clever one. We had always stuck together. You see, most of the things you are examined on are done in teams. Dwarf life is about working together. We made a good team too but then things went bad. In the last year, he tried to take the credit for everything we did. He wanted some special prize.

You know how fiercely competitive he is. Expecting me to toe the line and do his donkey work for him. Well, he was mistaken. I wasn't interested in prizes but wasn't going to be walked over."

"What was he trying to win, dad? I heard he blew his chance of being in the Royal Diggers and exploring far off mountains!" Himple knew a little of the story but never realised how much his dad was involved. His dad never spoke of his school days, so Himple paused, "Please carry on, dad!" "When he had to choose where to aim his axe, assess the stone, look for flaws and lines of weakness, he just didn't do so well without me. Before he knew it, he was an average student and destined to go nowhere. I graduated and went to the Animal Dept. in the Royal Mountaineers. He stayed on at the academy where he eventually became a master. He blames me Himple, and he is taking it out on you!" His dad let go of his beard and beat the fence post with his fist.

"RRRRRRRR!" Within seconds Mabel had positioned herself between Himple and his dad. "Steady Girl!" Himple stood and stroked Mabel as his retreating dad looked a little scared. "I have never known a buggane like her. She is getting very attached to you." "Could I take her out, just for a while? Let her play in the woods; she would love it!" Himple never missed a chance to ask but knew the answer...

He knew the danger. Safety was vital to keeping animals especially ferocious creatures.

The answer had always been a flat and an instant no. His dad looked up at Mabel. "If there was somewhere we could take her with no one around, let's think about it." Inside Himple exploded...the possibilities...where, when, how...must be somewhere...

Mabel

Chapter Three: The Stones

Barnaby met Himple at the Realm Gateways. This was their plan every morning. It was the least crowded way into the academy and the most unlikely one to be dwarfed by (manned by) a patrolling Grimtrunk. Grimtrunk hated gateways and travel of all kinds. Barnaby looked very upset. "My parents say if I don't pass this year, they are going to give me to the circus and tell everyone I ran away!" Barnaby poured out his emotions at Himple. Barnaby looked very stressed. He grabbed his axe like it was a comfort blanket and sank to the floor.

Himple pulled on his beard like his father did, searching for something to say to calm his friend. He looked at the Circle of Stones. The giant rectangular doorways joined with rocks on top of them. It was what Stonehenge would have looked like before it got knocked down by giants, but that was a story for another day and there was a good reason not to play with balls inside a monument. "We can do it, Barnaby, we just need a plan, and we need to help each other!" said Himple placing his hand on Barnaby's shoulder.

Barnaby smiled, lifted his massive frame, and followed Himple into the class for the day.

There was lots of excitement everywhere in the building, with huddles of dwarfs chatting. Something had happened, and there was a lot of commotion and fuss. The main area of activity was around the academy notice board. With the help of Barnaby's formidable bulk, they pushed their way to the front to see what was going on.

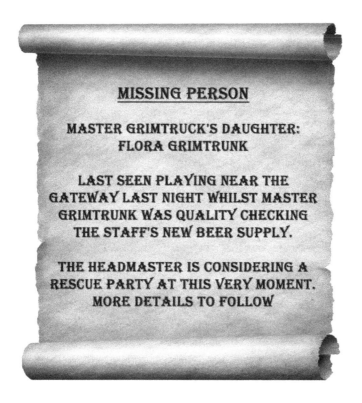

MISSING PERSON

MASTER GRIMTRUCK'S DAUGHTER:
FLORA GRIMTRUNK

LAST SEEN PLAYING NEAR THE GATEWAY LAST NIGHT WHILST MASTER GRIMTRUNK WAS QUALITY CHECKING THE STAFF'S NEW BEER SUPPLY.

THE HEADMASTER IS CONSIDERING A RESCUE PARTY AT THIS VERY MOMENT. MORE DETAILS TO FOLLOW

"'Blooming beards!!!' I would not want to stand in the way of old Grimtrunk getting her back. I bet he is worried," said Himple. "And we have him in our first session too!!!" said Barnaby.

Much to the relief of the whole class, Master Tumford arrived in place of Master Grimtrunk and fielded questions from the class that ranged from kidnapping to dragon fodder.

The bottom line was they were not sure which of the stone arches in the gateway she went through. Therefore, they were unsure of her destination. The dwarf students were unsure what would happen, but they all realised time was of paramount importance as the little dwarf was in a strange realm and more than likely edging away from the gateway.

Master Tumford was a good teacher and one of Himple's favourites. He was doing his best to calm the class when there was a knock on the door, and a very scared and out of breath first-year student ran in with a message for the master. There were whispers followed by an announcement by Master Tumford... "We must all gather in the Great Hall. Himple, Barnaby, Gwynfor and Jakob, please take your axe, armour and an emergency mission travel bag with you." "What is going on Himple?" Barnaby looked like he had seen a ghost as he asked his friend. "I am not sure, but axes and armours do not sound good. Maybe we are going to be used as target practice for Grimtrunk's anger management!" The Headmaster and Grimtrunk stood in front of the whole academy, and the Headmaster cleared his throat. "Teams will be formed to travel through each of the gateways on a quest to save the child. Each team will need a master and a couple of adult staff or, due to lack of numbers, a few very strong final year dwarfs. Our main concern is the lack of knowledge of the gateway. Even some of our best masters lack this knowledge. Himple, you, I am told, are, without doubt, the most knowledgeable student in this discipline for many years, so you will team up with a master with little knowledge." "Yes Sir," Himple said with a mixture of fear and excitement.

So as far as dreams coming true, Himple was just beginning travelling to a far-off realm. Adventure, discovery and danger. However, his dream soon became a nightmare when the teams were announced.

"Anyone but Grimtrunk, anyone but Grimtrunk, anyone but Grimtrunk," Barnaby whispered to Himple, who nodded in agreement.

The Headmaster reeled off the names, "Master Grimtrunk, our groundsman, Mr Podwick, with young Barnaby and Himple as the Realm Expert." "OOOOOOO!" Barnaby said, but fortunately, this was anticipated by Himple, who put a hand over his mouth.

Before they knew it, they were kitted out with the latest survival gear and supplies and were at the gateway. Grimtrunk was grumpy, to say the least, and was eager to go but not before he insulted his team. "Well, they have lumbered me with the worst team imaginable, bumbling Barnaby, wimple Pimple and podgy Podwick. Talking of Podwick, where is he?"

Just then, there was a commotion, and Podwick entered in armour that was at least two sizes too small and a very large rusty axe that had seen better days. "Here, Master Grimtrunk. Sir, took a little longer than I thought to get the old kit on and find old Betty, my battle axe, but I am here and ready for action!" At which point he tripped, rolled into a perfect ball and cannoned across the courtyard and knocked 20 dwarfs flying before landing at Himple's feet.

"Here, sir, let me help you up," said Himple. "That's a very kind young dwarf, but I am nobody's sir. Call me Pod." Podwick adjusted his small round glasses with a broad smile across his face as Himple and Barnaby helped him to his feet.

The Headmaster hurried across and gave each of the masters a piece of parchment which they opened. It had a gateway number on it and instructions of what to send back through if they needed help. "We are gate four. Look after this like your life depended on it!" said Grimtrunk passing the note to Himple.

Himple turned to Barnaby, "The South Americas," Himple activated the gateway impressing Grimtrunk for the first time ever and through they went.

19

Barnaby and Himple

Chapter Four: The Foreign Realm

"Flora! Flora! Flora!" Grimtrunk shouted, "Sir, stop! We must assess the area and make sure it is safe first..." said Himple in a panic. Grimtrunk grunted and started to look around. They were by what looked like a relic of an old stone temple, covered in vines and foliage. It was hot and humid.

Grimtrunk was just manically looking around. Himple began to think sending him was a mistake. He was naturally desperate to find Flora, but Himple was worried it would impair his judgement. On the other extreme to manic searching was Pod, who sat next to a herbaceous border looking at the plant life. "Sir...Master Grimtrunk, do we need a plan? Where are we going to search?" asked Himple.

"Plan...Plan...yes well..." Grimtrunk's clueless ramblings were interrupted by Barnaby. "Look at the footprints and some material caught on this branch!" Himple looked. He was right. "Trolls! Sir, I would say big ones too. What colour dress was Flora wearing?" Himple looked at the yellow material on the branch and hoped Grimtrunk's daughter hated yellow. He hoped she was wearing another colour, and they were not the team with the task of bringing her home. They could have had a quick look around and return home in time for tea. Grimtrunk stood in silence, tugging on his beard. "Yellow..." His words hurt Himple like an arrow in his side. There was silence. "We should go back and get reinforcements," said the worried Pod. Grimtrunk looked at the trio, "My daughter's life is in the hands of you three! It is very tempting. Himple will agree time is of the essence. If it is trolls, she could be in a pot by now with some veg."

Himple looked at the others. He wanted to return home but knew his master was correct. "We need to find her and fast", said Himple, turning to grab the parchment. He found a small white stone to be sent as a coded message. He threw the stone through the active gateway, and the four dwarfs headed off in the same direction as the trolls' footprints.

"That was a really good spot, Barnaby. Keep your eyes open for any more clues," said Himple. "Master Grimtrunk, are trolls difficult to fight?" Himple asked. "… I'm not sure, I don't think... that is I have never...Well, what I am meaning to say is..." Grimtrunk stuttered. "Tricky devils, fight dirty, sharp swords but very poor reach and badly made metal. Keep a good distance and hit their sword or dagger hard with your axe. Keep a low base. You get good power then." Pod spoke like an expert master in axe skills. In one short sentence, he taught the young dwarfs more than Grimtrunk had in years.

"What makes you an expert in trolls?" Grimtrunk asked. Groundskeeper Podwick looked embarrassed at himself, letting go and talking like that. He apologised, "Beggin' your pardon, master, just remembering my days in the Army. I wasn't always a groundsman. I spent 60 years in the Royal Mountain Guards...Me and old Betty picked up a thing or two about trolls and a keen dislike of them, too, if you don't mind me saying". Grimtrunk didn't reply but looked impressed. Barnaby couldn't help but saying something, "Well, blooming beards, who would have thunk it! Pleased you're with us, Pod!" "Master Grimtrunk...Sir?" Himple tried to get the attention of his master. "What is it? We need to move quicker. You are all slowing me down!" Grimtrunk grumbled. Himple tried again, "Sir...realm investigation class advises we climb trees to get a good view and assess the landscape. These are good trees to climb, I think." "Philodendron Vines, young man, that's what you are looking at climbing up those coconut trees, makes them ideal for climbing", Pod said. Grimtrunk huffed and ordered, "Barnaby...tree...now!" Himple couldn't help thinking of just how useful Pod was and how underestimated he had been. His dad had been right about Grimtrunk rather unimpressive and not a leader.

"There is a mountain ahead covered in trees. Someone has a big fire on the top. I can see this path leading to the mountain. There are other clearings, a big one at the bottom of the mountain. There is a clearing about 10 minutes' walk from here…" Barnaby scrambled back down, having given them the news.

Everyone looked at Grimtrunk, who stared into nothingness. Himple grabbed his axe and pack and said, "Come on, let's see what's along this track then". They could smell smoke as they approached the clearing. There was a well-trampled area of ground with the remnants of a large fire in the centre. Himple and Barnaby checked the perimeter and looked for a piece of evidence to help with the search. Pod was looking at a bush with bright yellow flowers near a pathway. "The little girl's dress was yellow, right?" said Pod. "Yes, yes, she loves yellow, anything yellow", Grimtrunk said, sounding increasingly upset. "There is a large handful of yellow flowers missing from this bush," Pod announced. Himple was there like a shot, "Trolls hate flowers. They are practically allergic to them. I wonder if Flora managed to grab some on the way past?"

The group followed the path for any more signs of the troll pack...

Meanwhile, back at the academy...

"Stone, Headmaster, through Master Grimtrunk's Gateway!" the young dwarf darted into the Headmaster's study. "Stone? Stone! What colour? What colour, young dwarf?" "Mmm white, sir ... White", the young dwarf said, looking absolutely terrified.

Just then, there was a loud knock on the door, and Himple's father came in and started ranting before he could be welcomed. "You sent my son to *mountain knows where* without so much as thinking about telling me! He is hardly old enough to leave the house, never mind to be allowed through a gateway on a mission. Where is he? Who's with him, and when is he coming back?!" Horace Gwim, as you can imagine, was completely livid but did not get the opportunity to get a reply from the Headmaster as he was followed into the room by a king's guardsman, who it has to be said was equally annoyed, "May I remind you that any unauthorised gateway travel needs reporting to your local squadron and under subsection 5 of the Realm Code and I quote, for rescue missions of any type cannot be made without a member or appointed military dwarf present'. I also inform you that due to this transgression, all use of the gateway is hereby forbidden until further notice." This was rebuffed by Horace Gwin, who said no jumped-up soldier was going to stop him from following and rescuing his son. Then, by the Headmaster, who said no one was going to tell him what to do in his academy. This was followed by a lot of dwarf shoving, shouting and beard pulling...

Flora

Chapter Five: Trolls

"Why would they want her? What has she done? Will they really eat her?" grumbled Master Grimtrunk. Himple followed through the forest. He wasn't sure if he should or not, and he wasn't sure what he could say to give his master any hope.

Himple picked up the courage and decided to reply, "Trolls in these parts are well known for trying to kill big beasts. They have been known to kill mountain ogres and giants, even dragons...." Grimtrunk looked up at Himple in sadness. "Himple, is that really true?" "Oh Yes!" said Himple, proud his master was talking to him and getting his name correct. "You see, they normally use small catches as bait to catch the bigger beasts..." Himple was practically steamrolled as Grimtrunk ran past shouting, "What! You what? Flora bait for a dragon!!!"

When they caught up with Grimtrunk, he was hidden behind a large bush. He beckoned them to be quiet and to join him in hiding. There, in a clearing ahead of them, was a group of trolls.

Himple pulled the flowers off the bush and started rubbing them on him. Grimtrunk growled under his breath at him, "What are you doing, you idiot?" "The trolls have an amazing sense of smell. Rub these on, or they will smell us

27

for sure", Himple said, passing around the highly scented white flowers. "Himple whispered, "Jasminum". "Clever young dwarf you have here, Master Grimtrunk!" "SSSSSShhhhhh!" the other three replied in unison.

From where they hid, they could clearly see a group of the most disgusting trolls you could ever wish to meet. The green warty creatures were lying around, wearing stolen armour and clothes with leather straps and bands wound around their arms and feet. The trolls loved to fight amongst themselves, especially over food.

Himple could see a few trolls that were rolling around on the floor. The larger trolls, three of them, were sitting on a rock.

"I say, we just eat her. She ain't big enough to tempt it out of that cave", said the largest fattest troll, Troggin. "We need to cut her, get her juices flowing that will get the old girl out of there!" said Trock, who was a tall troll with long fingers and nose. He looked the nastiest of them. The other troll just agreed with them both and looked worried. His name was Tungus.

"I don't like either of those options", said Barnaby quietly. "But where is she? I can't see her. Can you?" Grimtrunk whispered. They all looked out into the clearing, trying to spot Flora. It was obvious she was still alive. There was a silence from the band of trolls as Trock stood up, his imposing tall figure towering above them. "Make ready, you filthy band of scurvy scum!" "We head for the mountain and a good feed. Follow me!" With those words, Troggin somehow lifted his massive frame, and Trungus stood and turned around to face the mountain and follow his lead.

"There! There! On that one's back. Look!" said Himple. "Shhhhhhhhhhh," said the others, and then they spotted it in a backpack made of an old leather sack on Trungus' back. Grimtrunk sat and watched with mixed emotions. Part of him wanted to run after Flora and grab her, let her know he was there at the very least. The other realised to get her back was going to take planning.

For the first time, Grimtrunk took the lead, waiting for the pack of trolls to move out of sight down the track. He rose to his feet. "Right, we need a plan to separate Flora and that troll she is strapped to from the others. We need to stay close to them but not be spotted for now. If they are going to a cave, that means they may be heading to the mountain." Barnaby stood up, and like a soldier inspired by a mighty general, he replied: "Yes, sir and mountains are what us dwarfs do best!!" A smile crossed Grimtrunk's face. It was so unusual to see him smile. He was hardly recognisable.

29

What dwarfs were not good at was being quiet. What dwarfs were not good at was going for more than a few hours without a meal or a glass of beer. It was not true that dwarfs put mead or beer in their babies' bottles. They only started to give beer and mead to toddlers of 3 or 4. Before that, they gave babies a mixture of milk, honey and sherry.

The group were all hungry. Pod had managed to collect a few supplies before they left and had not missed the opportunity to stuff his bag with berries and mushrooms. "Here you go, Rum Rusks and Bumble Berries. That will keep you going." Pod seemed proud to be contributing. They all tucked in.

Himple was distant. He stared at the mountain, thinking about what laid in store for them.

Back at the academy...

Once the fighting and beard pulling was over, Horace Gwim, The Guardsman and Headmaster sat on the floor, frowning at each other. The Headmaster was first to his feet, "I have all but two of the search teams back. Only one communication and that was from Grimtrunk's team, who said they were investigating further, sent in pebble code. That is the team that Himple is with," the Headmaster confirmed. "Who else is in the group with Grimtrunk?" asked Himple's dad. "Grimtrunk chose them himself; he was quite insistent!" the Headmaster swallowed hard then continued, "Grimtrunk, Himple, Himple's friend Barnaby, and Groundsman Podwick." Horace Grim stood up, and if smoke actually came out of your ears like in a cartoon, it would have been happening there and then! You sent my son through to another realm with that idiot Grimtrunk, porky Podwick and another pupil, not even a good one!!!!!"

OK, well, let's just say that started off another batch of fighting and beard pulling. Just then, the door opened and in came another military type. Much older and very stern looking. He cleared his throat and stamped his war axe on the ground, "AAAAATTTEEENTION!!!!!!!

Get yourselves together, you lily-livered leprechauns. I have been informed by a more level headed individual what is going on, and I am amazed that you could not wait for some guardsman to accompany your staff and as for sending young dwarfs, well, whatever next.

They all knew him, The Brigadier. It was hard to give an equal position in our realm. He was a cross between a mayor, judge and general. He continued, "Matter of law dictates to us until we get further communication of safety, no further missions can be sent until the 4th day. At which time, it is a rescue mission for the search team. Until then, we sit, and we wait, and you, Headmaster, give good thought to making sure your teams are very strong in the future. No one dwarf follows them until I approve it. Do I make myself clear?"

Whilst they agreed, Horace Gwim had a look in his eye that he would not let this end here.

Back at camp, the team had finished eating. They were packed up and ready to follow the trolls. Himple had spotted a part of the mountain with no trees and dark areas that could be a cave. It looked very dark and scary, with mist rising upwards to cover its base. "I have an awful feeling that we are heading there," Himple pointed to the dark clearing. The others looked closely transfixed (that's like glued to looking at a thing). "We should go, follow me...", Grimtrunk said, and they headed out of camp.

Podwick

Chapter Six: Where Did That Lake Come From?

As they headed through the forest following the trolls, they noticed they were soon catching them up. Trolls had a very distinct aroma. Stink would be more accurate. If there was a word even smellier than stink, I would have used it.

Grimtrunk beckoned them to slow down and then to be quiet. They peeked through the trees to where two particularly large trolls sat on lookout duty. Their arguing was loud and well-timed as they could have easily stumbled straight into the clearing where they sat.

"Should we circle around them?" Barnaby asked in a whisper. "Just a little, let's see where the whole group is. There may be more of them", Grimtrunk replied and urged them to follow him. As they walked around, they found thick undergrowth and then the worst possible thing happened.

Crack! Pod had stood on a dead branch! It was such a loud noise; they all knew they would be heard. As the others hid, Himple reacted, searching in his bag for the bird food he liked to feed the canaries with back home. Himple, fast as you like, reached into his top pocket where he kept his all-purpose whistle. Bird impersonation was another of Himple's skills.

The trolls were up and heading in Himple's direction. He lifted the whistle and started a bird call. "That's not a bird call. What are you doing?" said Grimtrunk from behind a bush in a state of panic. Himple continued as the troll approached with their daggers drawn. Then, Himple changed the call to a bird call and threw the seeds as hard as he could towards the trolls. Then, his plan began to work: Firstly, birds started to dive in on the trolls to get the seeds, but then reacting to Himple's earlier call, Harpies attacked the birds and then, in turn, the trolls. Harpies, in case you didn't know, were like pixie-sized gargoyles with quite human faces, vicious and green with sharp teeth and bats wings. Imagine a swarm of miniature green flying witches without hats.

It was like swarming wasps around a jam pot. Harpies dive-bombing the trolls, each with a bird in the hand, taking bites from the trolls.

"Help! Get these orrible bug grabbers offa me!!" "Duck Burk, I'll whack it!" The trolls shouted at each other. The biggest troll grabbed his club and swung it, missing the nearest Harpy and bashing the other troll, Grub. He then grabbed his club and bashed the other troll back in revenge. Well, the trolls continued to bash each other as the Harpies nibbled at them. Himple and the others seized their opportunity, skirted around them and made for the path, keeping out of sight.

The team headed for a very large hollow tree to hide inside. Grimtrunk praised Himple, much to his surprise. "What next, sir?" asked Himple. "We need to get to that mountain, and if possible, beat the trolls there!" Grimtrunk's words inspired Pod to raise his fist in reply. Raising his fist, he made a hole in the tree above, getting his arm quite stuck above his head.

"Stuck, what do you mean stuck? Balding beards!" Grimtrunk was in full rant mode, losing the plot completely, grabbing Pod by the leg and pulling him. Barnaby, who was on watch outside, came in to help Himple and Grimtrunk pulled away at the groundkeeper's leg.

"What's going on in there, Burk?" shouted Grub, one of the large trolls who had found themselves outside the same tree as the dwarfs. Barnaby spotted them. "Master Grimtrunk, you better look!" Grimtrunk replied, "Not Now! Can't you see, I am trying to get this clumsy idiot out of this tree!" "But sir!" said Barnaby, the panic in his voice gaining everyone's attention.

The trolls had drawn their daggers and were approaching the tree. Burk replied, "I think we may just have found our supper; grab um!!!"

Now all good stories have cliff hangers, and this one is no different.

Let's catch up with the goings-on.

Back at the academy. (Sorry all)

Back in the realm of the academy Horace Gwim had returned home and told his wife everything, who was absolutely beside herself. In fact, she was so cross she had stopped cooking, cleaning and doing pretty much anything. This is unheard of for a dwarf lady and even more unheard of for Mrs Gwim.

They sat in silence until there was a knock on the door. Mrs Gwim would normally have answered it before the visitor had finished knocking, but not today. She sat there like she was frozen in time. Mr Gwim answered the door. It was a soldier dwarf saying he was an official messenger from the government. Horace signed for the message and returned to the table. Mrs Gwim burst into tears. "This is them, telling us he's dead, eaten by something horrible and foreign!" Horace opened the letter and lay it flat on the table.

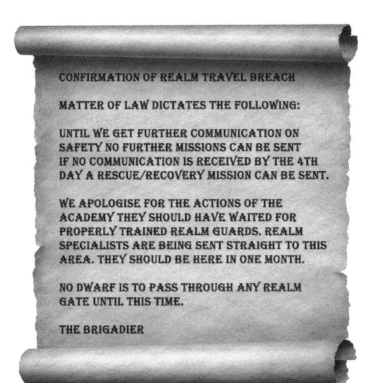

CONFIRMATION OF REALM TRAVEL BREACH

MATTER OF LAW DICTATES THE FOLLOWING:

UNTIL WE GET FURTHER COMMUNICATION ON
SAFETY NO FURTHER MISSIONS CAN BE SENT
IF NO COMMUNICATION IS RECEIVED BY THE 4TH
DAY A RESCUE/RECOVERY MISSION CAN BE SENT.

WE APOLOGISE FOR THE ACTIONS OF THE
ACADEMY THEY SHOULD HAVE WAITED FOR
PROPERLY TRAINED REALM GUARDS. REALM
SPECIALISTS ARE BEING SENT STRAIGHT TO THIS
AREA. THEY SHOULD BE HERE IN ONE MONTH.

NO DWARF IS TO PASS THROUGH ANY REALM
GATE UNTIL THIS TIME.

THE BRIGADIER

"Well, no wonder the Headmaster sent people for one month, but why Himple? He is just a young dwarf!" Mrs Gwim seemed to be coming to terms with things. "We would have wanted action if our child had gone through," she said.

Horace sat deep in thought, repeating the words over in his mind. No dwarf is to pass through. No dwarf is to pass through....How can we help the boy?

Now it is important to note that dwarfs do not break the rules. They are very organised and love routine. BUT........

they are also very cunning and good at working around the rules.

Back in a tree and in BIG trouble!

Barnaby joined the others and grabbed a leg. Himple shouted, "Pull you lot. Grimtrunk granny could pull harder than you!" With a massive laugh, Pod's arm came loose, and they all fell to the floor. There was a massive cracking noise from below as Pod tumbled down on the others. He hit them just as a giant hand reached into the hollow tree. As Pods' weight combined with the others, the floor gave way, and the dwarfs fell. Down and down they went. Himple could hear the trolls shouting after them. They seemed to fall for ages. There was just blackness around them, then the tunnel narrowed. Himple was the first to hit the narrowing using his legs and arms to slow himself down. The tunnel levelled out, and soon, they were skating on their bottoms like they were in tubes at a waterpark. Twisting and turning up and down, Himple could hear Grimtrunk gaining on him. Soon, they were together and hurtling towards a large opening. When they reached the opening, they flew out into fresh air and fell into an underground shallow lake. Grimtrunk got to his feet waist-deep in water and was hit from behind by Barnaby, knocking him back under the water. "You blithering idiot!" Grimtrunk ranted, as once again he stood up. Bang! Pod hit Grimtrunk from behind, this time sending him flying forward into the others. They all stood up, Grimtrunk last, and instead of being cross, he burst into fits of giggles. They all laughed together.

So they were underground, in a strange realm, not knowing where they were or how to get to the surface. Strangely, being dwarfs and being underground, they were at ease, relaxed and surprisingly happy.

Burk and Grub

Harpy

Chapter Seven: Locomotion

They investigated the large cavern with the lake in the centre that they found themselves in. Exits were leading away from the main cave, and one had what looked like an old railway track in it.

"I think this was a gem mine, but it looks disused for some time", said Himple looking more closely at the walls. "I think we should follow the track; maybe it heads for the mountain?" he continued.

Barnaby headed along the track to see what he could see, "There's a truck and torches down here", he shouted to the others, followed by Pod, who pulled a gadget from his pocket and lit two torches. The truck was the type with a see-saw like mechanism on the front that propelled the truck along the track. Like those seen in the American wild west, they are called handcarts. The dwarfs were well at home and started to mount the truck. "Look!" Grimtrunk was looking into the bucket on the back of the truck. "GEMS!" The base of the bucket was filled with hundreds of opals, rubies and emeralds of all kinds.

Everyone but Himple gathered around, filling their pockets and backpacks. "What's wrong with you? Come on, grab some!!" Grimtrunk snapped at Himple. "Well, I was just thinking, that's all?" Himple looked very concerned.

Grimtrunk had quickly learned that he needed to take note of Himple's "thinking's". However young he was and however mean he had been to him in the past, he was beginning to value the young dwarf. He raised his eyebrows in anticipation of Himple's explanation. Himple continued, "Well, I can't think of a single dwarf that would leave that amount of gems lying about. In fact, if there are this many gems around, why aren't there dwarfs mining them right now?"

As Grimtrunk and Himple were considering who or what had stopped the dwarfs from mining the gems, Pod decided to check the mechanism on the truck, reminiscing as he did. "Barnaby, my boy, I worked one of these long before you were born. Hard work it was; making sure this brake is fully off is the most important thing. You pull it up like this". Barnaby jumped on to look closer. Pod pulled the brake right up to show the young dwarf how it worked. The slope was enough to set the truck going, only aided by Pod falling backwards on the lever.

"Himple, quick! We are moving!!" Barnaby shouted. The truck shot off, and Himple and Grimtrunk set about their chase. Barnaby jumped into the bucket at the back of the truck. Reaching out, he grabbed hold of Grimtrunk's hand and pulled him in. They fell in a heap. Himple ran and ran. He managed to get two hands on the bucket when the track started to dive on a steeper decline. It was so fast now that Himple was flying behind the truck with both feet in the air like a superhero. He held on tight as if his life depended on it, which it probably did!

Down and down they went. The speed was such that it blew out one of the torches. Grimtrunk and Barnaby got to their feet as Pod tried to apply the brake. Sparks came streaming from the wheels like a firework! Barnaby grabbed Himple and pulled him in.

If this were a roller coaster, it would be closed for being far too dangerous. Well, it would appear they were heading for the mountain and probably the thing or things that had scared everyone away. The track levelled off and the speed reduced to only really fast, which goes to show how fast it had been going. Pod had given up on the break. Himple and the others had got to their feet as they zoomed toward another dark tunnel. Instead of another decline as they hit the next tunnel, they went up. The truck's momentum only slowed them a little as they climbed the track.

As they rose and rose, they came to a sharp incline, so sharp they had to hold on, and suddenly they realised that if they stopped going up, there was only one other direction they could go!

DOOOOO WWWNNN!!!!

Back at Himple's parents' house (sorry again)…

Mrs Gwim looked at the window and turned with a concerned look at her husband, "They are very unsettled. Will the fencing hold?" she asked. Himple's dad didn't answer but rose from his seat and made his way over to the window. With both hands on the window sill, he bowed his head and sighed. "They miss him as much as us, especially Mabel. Never seen an attachment like it. Not with any creature, especially not a wild, dangerous one. Why she would protect him against anything. (there was a silence) She would protect him from anything." Mr Gwim stood up, his face beaming with smiles for the first time since Himple went missing.

Back underground…

"Grab the lever!" shouted Grimtrunk, climbing to the front of the trunk. He and Barnaby took it in turns to push down the lever, trying to keep what little momentum they had, going for as long as they could. Up and down like a see-saw, the peak of the track was in sight. Barnaby showed his amazing strength pushing and pulling the lever. It was obvious Grimtrunk was struggling. Barnaby, all of a sudden, started to giggle. He looked at Grimtrunk, who was grimacing and sweating as he heaved the lever. "Come on, sir. Your Granny could do better than that!" Barnaby laughed. Grimtrunk joined in the laughter. The laughter gave them just the boost they needed to get them over the peak and to flat ground.

The truck came to a gradual halt with the help of the break. There was a smell of burning in the air, and the temperature had increased a lot since they got onto the truck.

Pod fully applied the brake, and Himple started to look around. There was pumice like texture on the outside of the tunnel walls. "The walls are quite volcanic. There has been considerable heat through here in the past", said Himple, and he continued, "There is no animal life or plant life for that fact." (Pumice is like a stone honeycomb)

Grimtrunk joined Himple in his inspection of the walls. It was hot in the tunnel. Grimtrunk rubbed his beard, "I don't think anything too scary would fit in these tunnels, but the sooner we get to the surface, the better. If there is volcanic activity, these tunnels could fill with lava very quickly."

"I think we will leave the truck and walk from here. We need to find an exit. It must be dark outside by now," Grimtrunk continued, picked up his things and started his trek down the track, followed by the others.

The Dwarf Handcart

Chapter Eight: The Mountain

The group had walked for a while when Himple stopped, "Shhhhhhhhhhh, I can hear water." The others stopped and listened. Just ahead was a small gap in the wall and the sound of water. Himple squeezed through and reported back, "It is an opening, and there is water coming down from above. The opening above seems large enough to climb through." "Ok, we will follow you," said Grimtrunk. Barnaby and Grimtrunk squeezed through with far more difficulty than Himple, who was thinner. Then came the problem. "What do you mean you're stuck!!"

Pod was halfway through and not going anywhere...

Now Grimtrunk, who had been rather relaxed in the last few hours, lost his temper. Being a family-friendly book I can not print all of what Grimtrunk said, "Breath in you xxx xxxxx xxxx xxx xxxx xxxxx xxxxxxx xxxx xxxx xxxxxx xxx xxx" You get the idea. Barnaby grabbed his axe and started at the wall. Fortunately, the pumice-like stone was quite weak, and Barnaby soon had Pod through.

"Up here!" shouted Himple, who had already climbed the wall and was entering the hole where the water poured out of.

"Not another hole! I really am the wrong shape for all of this!" said Pod as he started to climb.

Despite being very wet, the climbing wasn't too hard, and the gaps were okay for Pod to get through. As they gained height, there were more vines and roots to hold onto, but the stone surface of the shaft they were climbing was becoming soil-like and wet.

There was still no light to give them hope, but they soon found what they thought was the surface. They climbed out, and they were in a cave. It was still dark, but their eyes were more accustomed to it. They checked the perimeter and decided to rest; they couldn't remember when they last slept. They were exhausted.

Back at the academy...

There were two guards near the gateway and two at the main entrance. They changed every 30 minutes. The dwarf guards changed shift at 10 pm. The bush that Horace Gwim found himself in was not very comfortable, but he was armed with a flagon of ale and some very nice cheese and pickle sandwiches. He continued to make his notes long into the night...

Back in a cold corner of a cave, who knows where ...

Barnaby rolled over. He had been using Pod's ample tummy as a pillow and, in changing position, had fallen off, waking the others...

It was obviously morning, and their rest had turned to a night's sleep with none of them aware of the passing time. There was a dim light in one direction of the cave. It made shadows and shapes that played tricks on their eyes. They got themselves packed up and headed off towards the light. The cave opened out, and as they turned a corner, they could see daylight. It was quiet as they crept out of the cave and hid behind some bushes. The mountain was now in clear view, and they were close now, very close.

"Well, we have travelled some distance. I hope you are not planning on going back that way?" Pod said.

They all agreed they should avoid another truck ride. From the bush, they could see the mountain top with a trickle of smoke wisping into the sky. They had to be almost at the foot of the mountain now. There was a clear path ahead of them heading in the direction of the mountain; it all looked quiet for now.

The group headed for the trees along the pathway, cautiously looking out for trolls. They eventually reached the troll camp, and once again, Grimtrunk was relieved to see his daughter alive.

The camp was at the foot of the mountain with an area of stone-circled fire pits, some with large black cauldrons others with simple fires. There was an area with large table tree stumps that made stools. The trolls themselves were all asleep in an area off to the other side of the cave opening. There, in the centre of the sleeping trolls, was a cage, and in the cage was Grimtrunk's daughter, Flora. The cage hung not far from the ground, suspended from a tree branch. It was like a very large version of a canary or budgie cage you may find in the lounge of an old lady. "Could we sneak through without waking them?" Barnaby asked. Grimtrunk whispered his reply, "It would be very dangerous." "Let me try!" said Pod in an entirely too loud voice and headed off.

Well, even if this rescue was possible, Pod was the last person in the group with the appropriate talents for the mission. It would be like asking a nursery kid to play rugby for England or asking a sumo wrestler to do ballet! Anyway, it was too late. The chubby old gardener was already on his way, with Betty, his axe, ready for action.

"He's mad!" said Himple. "Brave!" said Barnaby. "A blithering idiot!" said Grimtrunk.

Well, by this time, he was halfway there. There were a number of the trolls sniffing in their sleep, smelling dwarf, one of their favourite meals. Each step was a triumph as he plodded through the sleeping, snoring and farting troll bodies. In case you have never had the misfortune of smelling a troll fart, they are the stinkiest thing you could imagine. Even skunks don't like the smell.

The cage was right in the middle of the bodies, and there was a heavy bolt on the cage door, but luckily no lock.

"The bolt's too high. How will he reach it?" Himple asked. "He will be troll breakfast by then!" said Grimtrunk, quite sure of Pod's imminent failure.

Then it happened. I couldn't say for certain what exact body part Pod tripped over. The stepped upon troll yelped and stood up, looking for who had woken him. In doing so, he stood on the troll next to him, who in turn stood up and punched him. Like a Mexican wave, the next troll woke and kicked or punched his neighbouring troll until all hell was let loose. There were fists and legs everywhere! Troll bodies on the floor. It was like a battle royal in wrestling with 40 giant wrestlers in the ring, only much smellier and far more biting and farting!

They couldn't see Pod anywhere. "He is very possibly in the belly of that big mean one who is standing in the middle with a club," said Grimtrunk, holding his head. As the fighting subsided and the trolls sat rubbing their bumps and bruises, the dwarfs could not believe their eyes. Flora was no longer in the cage.

"Has Pod got her?" asked Himple, looking around nervously. "We need to find them before these trolls realise she has gone!" Grimtrunk's panicked expression had returned. The three remaining dwarfs looked all around them to see any trace of Flora or Pod.

"There!" said an eagle-eyed Himple as he pointed toward the caves. "I don't believe it!" said Grimtrunk. Unbelievably, Pod was in the shadows of the cave entrance with Flora holding his hand. "However, did he do it?" asked Himple. "Dumb Luck!" said Grimtrunk. "He does smell a bit like a troll," said Barnaby, continuing, "That has to help..."

Grimtrunk gestured to Pod to wait there and hide while the dwarfs started to edge around the camp towards the cave.

There was a great deal of shouting coming from the trolls. Himple and the other made for the bushes and took a look. The tall, imposing troll camp leader Trock stood next to the cage, shouting and punching any troll that came near him. Then as clear as day, he shouted, "Find Her!"

At that point, Himple looked across towards Pod, who disappeared into the cave. "We need to get to the mountain before the trolls search these bushes," Himple whispered as loudly as he dared. The dwarfs set off keeping as low as they could. They could hear the approaching trolls.

Grimtrunk

Chapter Nine: Inside The Mountain

Back at Himple's house…

"Mabel! Mabel! Here, girl..." Mr Gwim's attempts to get Mabel to eat, drink or follow him were failing. "Can we try some of your porridge, Mrs Gwim? I have to get Mabel to move and follow me!" said Mr Gwim, now sounding desperate.

Back at the mountain…

"We're surrounded", whispered Barnaby. They were close to the base of the mountain but still a considerable way away from the cave entrance, where they last saw Pod and Flora.

"We've had it," said Grimtrunk with his head in his hands. "Done for, doomed, lost". Grimtrunk's woes were cut short by Himple's hand over his mouth. "There!" Himple pointed, "On the rock over there, an olm." "A what?" said the others. "The white lizard!" Himple said, rising to his feet, "Trust me! Follow me!"

The dwarfs jumped to their feet and followed Himple. They looked to be in the clear when a troll stood between them and the olm. "Between his legs", shouted Himple, and they slid right under his grasp and through his legs. The olm or cave salamander disappeared with the noise of the approaching dwarfs who followed the salamander into the bushes and down a small cave hole and into the mountain.

The cave was narrow and wet. They pushed themselves through with great effort. They could hear shouting from the entrance to the tunnel behind them and knew they had to keep going. Himple found it easy being less round than the others, but he could not see where he was going. It was so dark and smelled of egg, rather unpleasant egg at that. The slimy green algae in the tunnel was a godsend and helped the two larger dwarfs to slide along. Grimtrunk's backstroke technique pushing himself along would have been hysterical to watch if only it wasn't so dark.

They continued to crawl, front crawl or back crawl, along the small tunnel until Himple felt the opening widen and the water deepened. "Hold on!" he shouted to the others. Himple edged through the deeper water until he could feel another tunnel above his head. "Time to climb I think?" he asked the others who grunted and followed. There were vines and stones to hold, but some were loose. Soon they were all climbing. "Sorry!" shouted Himple as a stone fell, missing Barnaby and hitting Grimtrunk clean on the head. "Watch it!" he shouted. "Sorry!" shouted Himple again, "I mean watch out, I mean sorry!" It was too late. Once again,

Grimtrunk headed a rock. He was not best pleased. "That's it! I'm going first!" said Grimtrunk. There was, of course, no room for them to cross. "Light, I can see light", Himple was so excited he climbed faster up the tunnel until he reached a high ledge on the cave wall overlooking the main cave entrance where Pod and Flora were last seen. When all three dwarfs were on the ledge, they looked around for signs of life. They couldn't see the opening of the cave, but there was enough light to know they were near to the entrance. Strangely, no trolls were searching inside. "They've caught them already," Grimtrunk said, fearing the worst.

Himple concentrated on the positives and viewed the cave meticulously from high up on the cave wall. Barnaby was searching his pockets for food, and Grimtrunk was feeling sorry for himself. "How did you know there would be an escape route by the white lizard thing?" Barnaby asked Himple. "It was an olm; they are cave dwellers, white as they rarely see the sun." Barnaby smiled at his friend, proud of his knowledge.

Himple methodically checked the tunnel. There were several nooks and dark shadowy recesses. There was an area high up level with them that was like another balcony overlooking the main cave. The floor of the cave was rocky, half a stone-like grey colour and half a shiny green and yellow colour. There was no sign of Flora or Pod, and Himple did not dare to shout out to find them. He reached down and grabbed a pebble the size of a ping pong ball and threw it down to see if it caught the attention of his friends. The pebble hit the shiny green floor but didn't really bounce. Much to Himple's surprise, he noticed the whole green side of the floor wriggled and then sat still. "Did you see that?" said Himple, confused at what his own eyes had shown him. Neither were looking, and neither replied to Himple.

As Himple mulled over the idea of climbing down to investigate, three of the largest trolls entered the cave. They were holding large and very long spears. The others were now paying attention. The trolls shouted, "Little tasty thing, where are you? Come out!". They looked around, but one always stood at the front with a spear ready. "What are they doing?" asked Grimtrunk. "Why the spears? Trolls like daggerBBCs", added Barnaby. "I'm not sure, but I think there is something off with the green floor," said Himple.

They all peered over the ledge, being careful not to be seen. There was some more shouting, and then trolls could be seen arguing among themselves. "You do it! I did it last time!" said one of the others who looked scared. Finally, after much arguing, Burk, the large troll from the tree yesterday, entered. The trolls laughed at each other and called Burk over. They gave him a spear and retreated to the edge of the cave. Himple could not see them but heard a shout of "Now!" as Burk stabbed the spear at the green rock.

The green lumpy shiny rock wasn't a rock at all. It lifted in the air knocking Burk to the ground. It swished around, knocking the walls of the cave, just missing the dwarfs' high vantage point. "What was that?" asked Grimtrunk. Himple slowly moved backwards. Only when he was out of sight did he reply.

"It's a dragon's tail!"...

Himple's Mum

Chapter Ten: Dragons

The relationship between dwarf and dragon is an age-old one and one that has mainly been heated, if you pardon the pun. Both have a love for mountains, and neither likes to share. Dragons are complicated creatures. Most people in our realm will think of a T-rex with wings flying around breathing fire. There are many types of dragons often used to guard great treasures. They are chained up and treated badly. In the main, they seek a simple life and, with a good feed, will sleep for many, many years. Himple, as you would expect, was quite the expert.

The tail came to a stop, and Himple edged forward. "A Mboi Tata by the look of the yellow and green marking, quite a rare dragon," Grimtrunk and Barnaby looked blankly at him. "Is that good?" asked Grimtrunk. "No dragon is good, but this one could be worse. It hates the light and can't see well in it. It is more of a giant snake in appearance, with no arms, often small underdeveloped wings and legs, and it rarely flies". Flora and Pod were still nowhere to be seen. "The only answer with the trolls outside the cave is that the others have gone deeper in. If it's dark, they are in real danger of walking into a dragon." Himple looked concerned. Grimtrunk composed himself. "We need to go deeper in the cave. I can't ask you to come with me as it is more dangerous than imaginable. We are days from the rescue team arriving.

I suggest you find food and sit tight." Himple looked at Barnaby, "I can't speak for my friend, but I think we should stick together." Barnaby considered the situation and spoke, directing his words of great wisdom in the direction of Master Grimtrunk, "You are normally horrible to us, but you've not been all that bad these last few days. If Himple thinks we should stick together, then that's good enough for me."

Grimtrunk's head dropped. "I am sorry about the way I treat you both. I have been unfairly punishing you for my past regrets with Himple's dad." Grimtrunk continued, "I saw the special thing that Horace and I had in you two, and I guess it reminded me of my mistakes with your dad and all the things we could have done together. We were good friends until I messed things up..." Himple got to his feet. There was no sign of troll or tail movement now. "That is in the past. Saving your daughter and getting home is all that matters", Himple said, getting his pack and starting to edge along the shelf like a walkway high in the cave.

Deeper and deeper into the cave, they went still climbing and walking when possible on the ledges on the cave wall. The light grew dimmer the further from the cave entrance they got. The stones that dropped as they moved did not appear to attract the attention of the dragon. Himple being the lightest by some margin, found the climbing easy, but the other two were struggling. By now, they were past the tail, and the wider back of the dragon was just possible to see. The cave had widened, and there was a rabbit warren of small caves on the opposite side to Himple's position. They found a suitable ledge to rest and plan. There was no way to the other side to explore the small caves without going over the dragon. "Should we risk shouting for Pod?

The trolls won't hear us from here", Grimtrunk suggested. "The dragons might!" said Barnaby, not liking the idea. "If we were over that side, we could hide in those small caves. Pod and Flora may already be there", Himple suggested.

There was silence for a while as the three looked and planned in the darkness. "I have it up there! There, on the roof of the cave, is a raintree root system. The wood is very tough, so if we tie our small ropes together and attach the axe, then throw the axe into the tree root, we could swing across", Himple made it sound simple.

Grimtrunk's skill with an axe was legendary, but it was a very tricky task. Grimtrunk tied every knot like his life depended on it (which it probably did, by the way) and prepared for the throw. It was unlikely he would get another go. "Is there enough rope?" Barnaby asked with fear still growing, "We need to be ready to swing straight away in case we wake the dragon." Grimtrunk's hand shook as he held the axe. He passed the end of the rope to Barnaby. "Hold that very tight", he said.

Grimtrunk's practice swings looked troubled and far from confident, and then he let fly, and the axe was sent into the darkness. Would it hit the raintree root?

Back at the buggane enclosure…

"Horace, what are you doing with Himple's pyjamas? If Mabel eats them, I will be very, very cross!" said Mrs Gwim.

"Mabel could smell Himple on the pj's, and for the first time since Himple left, she came to the fence. The buggane was drawn to the scent. The rhino-sized panda/mole cross was a sight to behold at the best of times. Today, there was sadness in her eyes as Mabel held out a paw for Himple's pj's", Horace with fear in his eyes, opened the enclosure and led Mabel away, following Himple's scent into the darkness.

Back in the cave...

The axe hit the tree root with great precision, and Barnaby pulled hard to check it was secure. They grabbed the rope, all three of them. Dwarfs are not known for athletic feats, and I have to say one at a time may have been a safer approach. However, they swung, and it was going very well until halfway across, Barnaby lost his grip.

"Help!" shouted Barnaby as he plummeted downwards. Both Grimtrunk and Himple looked down in despair as Barnaby fell. On reflection, them losing concentration was an error as whilst looking down Himple and Grimtrunk hit the wall on the other side. THUD! They slid down the wall, landing in a seated position on the floor like two people sitting on a bus! "Don't just sit there. RUN!!" Barnaby shouted as he ran past them into the small cave exit. The dragon moved and lifted. That was enough to get Himple and Grimtrunk to their feet as they followed Barnaby into the cave.

They ran into a smaller cave that was not a quarter of the height of the main cave; it was, however, still as large as the size of a double-decker bus. It was dark and wetter than the main cave, and it was on a slope that led downward. Barnaby was nowhere to be seen. The two turned to look behind them. The dragon wouldn't fit in this space. It was much too small but given a chance, it could fill it full of fire. There was no sign of the dragon. "Barnaby!" Himple called, trying not to be too loud. The darkness was pierced by two eyes ... "Barnaby? Is that you?" Grimtrunk called ... There was no reply, then the words broke the silence, "Daddy, it's me!"

Flora burst towards them, her arms wide open. Grimtrunk fell to his knees. He couldn't hold back the tears anymore. They hugged so tightly, the tears rolling down their faces. Dwarfs rarely cried, even dwarf babies, but no one cared. Himple welled up too.

Himple looked down at them. It made the struggle so far worthwhile. Then he felt an arm on his shoulder. "Missed Me?" said Pod. "Look who I found", said Barnaby, grinning and feeling very proud of himself.

The group was together. "We did it!" said Grimtrunk, "I can't thank you all enough." Himple brought them back down to earth, "Well, that's the easy bit. We now need to get past a dragon and pack of bloodthirsty trolls and find our way back to the gateway to our realm".

Will Himple's Dad Find a Way to Help Him?

Chapter Eleven: Darkness

"There are more caves down there, but the water does get deep. I found some interesting root systems. There may be a way out", Pod explained. "Dragon and trolls or caves and water? Caves get my vote," said Himple.

They set off into the darkness, Pod leading the way weaving them through tunnels and caves. With very little to see, it was hard to get their bearings. "We need to get to the other side of the mountain. That is our best chance of escape," Grimtrunk said, looking ahead into the gloom. After an hour of trekking knee-deep in the water, they came to a large opening. As the time passed, they saw more and more as their dwarf eyes got used to the dark. They crept up to the opening. It was brighter, and as they peered around, they saw light from a crack high on the wall of the far side of the cave. "An exit, for sure. I think we will fit through," said Pod. The dwarfs were all studying the cave roof above them when Himple's eye caught another shape in the gloom. "What's that?" he asked, looking to the left of them into a large dark expanse of the cave. It looked like a fire, a large bonfire, but it appeared for a second and then it would go.

They returned their focus to the task of climbing to the cave top to escape. "We could use the vines if they are strong enough, but if not, it will be axe and rope to the top. We will need to climb down to cross to the far side of the cave before we can start our ascent," said Grimtrunk.

Himple caught the glow again. "I can see something from over there, like a fire," Himple said to the others. "Are you sure, young dwarf?" asked Pod as he and the others looked into the darkness. Then there was a cough, a cough as loud as a thunderstorm. Two fires could be seen in the gloom of the cave, and then it happened—a burst of fire across the cave right in front of them. The dwarfs dived for cover, and Grimtrunk hid Flora under them. When the flames ceased, smoke filled the air. The flames had opened the crevice above them, and a spear of light shone through the smoke like a giant torch was being pointed from above. As the smoke cleared, the beam of light revealed the origin of the flames, the dragon, Mboi Tata.

A Mboi Tata, to any of us not an expert like Himple in mythical creatures, is a dragon of ancient South American heritage. It could be described best as a giant snake with the head of a dragon, with eyes that glow like fire in an orange haze. Due to its lack of useful legs and arms, it has been known to swim in volcanoes and deep mountain lakes. Himple could see that this one was old and possibly sick. Around the thick spikes and horns of its neck were chains. Himple couldn't be sure the chains were secured, but they had been in place for years as they had worn away at the dragon's thick skin. "I don't know why but I think it's sad. I can feel her wisdom and sadness somehow," said Himple. "A killing machine, that's what it is!" snapped Grimtrunk.

"I'm going to take a closer look!" said Himple, and he marched off toward the dragon, axe and bag in hand.

Back at the academy, Realm Gates...

"Stop!!!!! Stop!!!!" the guardsmen shouted as they ran towards Horace Gwim. "What are you doing?" shouted the guard. "Get away from there!" shouted the other guard. Horace Gwim just smiled.

"Come with us!" said the senior guard, and then he took Mr Gwim into the academy. Much to the Headmaster's annoyance, he was sharing his grand office with one of the Brigadier's top generals. The unfortunately named General Groanbottom.

"What's this all about? What is the matter here?" said Groanbottom. He raised his extremely large body to a standing position, pulled his regimental uniform into place and walked towards Horace. "We found him snooping around the gateways, sir", said the guardsman. "Interloper, up to no good! Who are you?" Groanbottom said as he paced forwards and backwards in front of Mr Gwim. Horace said nothing, still feeling quite pleased with himself. "This is a very anxious parent whose son is part of the group that has not returned", said the Headmaster, coming to Horace's defence. Groanbottom continued, still pacing, "Lost your tongue, have you, interloper? Trying to get through the gate, and we stopped you, hey?" There was silence, and Himple's dad replied, "Just concerned for my son and thought I would come and look at the gates."

"Likely story, interloper. I remember the day when…

(In an effort to save the environment, I will not bother to recount to you the next hours of anecdotes from the General. Needless to say, he enjoyed the sound of his own voice far more than others did.)

Back in the cave…

"Himple stop!" shouted Grimtrunk as the young dwarf climbed down towards the dragon. Himple needed to see the dragon, not only because the giant serpent-like creature fascinated him but because Himple thought the creature was hurt or mistreated, and however dangerous the creature was, this could not be allowed.

"I'll go after him," said Barnaby, grabbing his axe, but both Grimtrunk and Pod held him back. "The only chance he has is not being detected by the beast now. If you go bumbling and bashing after him, the noise will get you both eaten," said Pod putting a reassuring hand on Barnaby's shoulder.

Himple reached the ground level, and he could feel the breath of the dragon as it slept. Himple crept forward, clinging to the side of the cave like he was on the top of the mountainside in a storm. He could now make out the shape of the dragon's nose.

It was big, so big he could've walked into its nostril and had a look around. Himple wanted to check the dragon's neck. Then the giant dragon's eye opened. It was like someone waking you up by shining a torch in your face. Himple almost felt like it burnt his skin. It was so hot and bright. Himple stood like a statue. Lots of larger creatures reacted to movement. Rather than just pure sight, he hoped if he stood absolutely still, he would avoid detection.

The eye shut, and Himple felt like his eyes had been blinded by the light. What little he could see in the darkness of the cave had disappeared. He let out a deep sigh. He stepped forward scared, reaching out in front of him as he walked. When his hand touched the dragon, he pulled it away as fast as he could. There was no reaction from the Mboi Tata dragon. Himple touched it again, this time gently. He was actually touching a dragon! The skin was smooth like interlocking china dinner plates with horny lumps between them.

Then it happened…

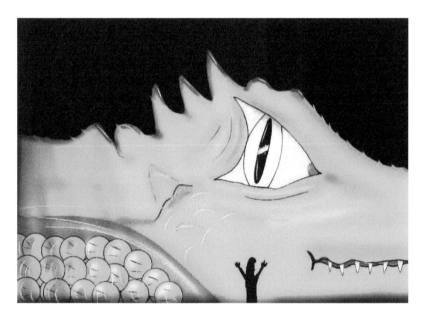

Himple and Moira

Chapter Twelve: Moira

At first, Himple was not sure if the voice was "out loud" or in his head. The minute he pulled his hand away from the dragon, it stopped. He had, of course, read that the most powerful of mythical creatures possessed a telepathic ability. Telepathy is the ability to think a message, talk brain to brain without a sound. The message Himple received was simple.

"Help me. My name is Moira."

Himple had never used telepathy before and didn't know anyone who had. He picked up courage and touched the dragon. *"I am Himple",* he thought. He waited, had it worked? Your brain did not give read receipts or turn the message to green. How would he know if he had sent a telepathic message?

"Help me, Himple". Himple let go to compose himself, "Oh gosh! Oh gosh!" he was thinking. Himple took a deep breath and reached out again. *"How can I help you?"* Himple thought.

"Break my chains! Set me free!"

Himple was cautious by nature, and he thought to himself without letting go of Moira. He was concerned this was a trick, and if he let her free, he would be toast or at least supper....

"I am not tricking you. You must trust me, I beg you!"

For Himple it came down to instinct, his love of animals, and good nature overcoming any fear. *"I will help you, Moira. I will set you free."*

From the darkness, Himple reached for his axe and followed the chain with his hands. The chain was very thick, so Himple knew there was no hope of breaking it. The end of the chain was bolted to the rock in two places. Himple was struggling to see a weak area of the rock to hit. He felt Moira move. She brushed against Himple, coiling herself, then she opened her eye, illuminating the rock side. Himple gripped his axe and struck the rock. It was hard. The axe bounced off the surface, and stinging vibrations shook Himple's hands and arms. He struck again and again. Not a blemish. Himple sighed.

"Need a hand?" came a voice from the darkness. Barnaby appeared with an axe in hand. Himple smiled. "Thanks!" he said, "This is Moira. She needs our help." Barnaby looked at Himple. "Talk dragon now, do you?" he said, chuckling. Barnaby struggled. The rock was hard. Himple examined the stone face in detail, following the lines

73

and minerals within it. "Here!" he said, pointing way above the chains. Barnaby swung. He managed to weaken it. Himple touched Moira.

"Almost there", Himple thought. "Where are the others?" he asked. "Heading for the daylight, I said we would catch up with them. They weren't happy I came after you," said Barnaby.

Barnaby was striking the second bolt in the rock time after time, with little joy. Himple examined the area closely as Barnaby took a well-deserved rest. He felt with his hands there was a crack above the bolt. Himple pointed it out to his friend. Barnaby raised his axe again and hit it at the first time of asking. The rock split, and the bolt fell. "Well done! Himple" and he turned to Moira.

Himple reached out… *"You are free!"*

"Climb on my neck when I break free. I don't want to squash you against the rocks."

Himple and Barnaby started to climb the scaly, shiny, horny skin of the dragon. "Are you sure about this?" questioned Barnaby as they climbed. They got to the larger spinal horns of the neck and held on tight.

"We are safe but watch out for our friends. They are climbing for the opening high in the cave side", Himple thought, worrying about the others.

Moira replied in an instant, *"Not safe. Trolls!"*

Moira groaned as she reached up for the first time in longer than she could remember. As she pulled, the chains fell from her neck like a cruise liner dropping anchor. Grimtrunk and Pod with Flora on his back had reached the opening. Himple could see their silhouettes against the bright sunlight outside the cave. Moira pushed forward, with Himple and Barnaby holding on tight, but it was too late. As they looked up, they could see trolls surrounding Grimtrunk and Pod. By the time Moira reached the opening, there was no sign of the dwarfs. Barnaby climbed out and looked around. They were gone.

Himple held on to Moira. *"I need your help now. Can you help me rescue my friends?"*

Himple heard a giggle from Moira as the dragon much looked forward to some troll payback time, and then she thought back. *"Hold on tight. It will be my pleasure!!!"*

Moira turned like a snake curling before an attack. The dwarf's grips were tested as they held onto the scales. The dragon weaved through the caves of the mountain until they were heading toward the opening. The trolls with their long spears were guarding the entrance. The same spears they had poked and tortured Moira with were waiting for her. As the trolls saw Moira's eye's like two fireballs, they shouted.

"Why aren't they running?" asked Barnaby. "I would!" Himple turned to face his friend and replied. "They think she is still chained up!" Barnaby laughed. "Of course, they are in for a BIG surprise!" Outside in the troll camp, there was pushing and pulling as Grimtrunk was tied to a large post. Somehow, they had put Pod and Flora in the hanging cage.

"Give me back my axe, and I will teach you a lesson!" shouted Grimtrunk. As you may well imagine, Master Grimtrunk was very cross. That does not do it justice. He was fuming!!! Two of the biggest trolls lifted Grimtrunk up above their heads and put him and the post he was tied to on the spit above the fire. The trolls then started to argue over the correct seasoning for a dwarf as poor Grimtrunk was rotated by another troll working the handle.

The argument continued until there was a cascade of screams, followed by troll bodies being thrown from the cave opening. This sent all the trolls into panic as Moira roared when she hit the daylight. What a sight as Moira's majestic head appeared, raised up, the silvery-green scales glistening in the sunlight.

Some of the trolls grabbed spears and charged, while others dashed for cover. As more of Moira's large snakelike body hit the daylight, the sheer magnitude of the dragon was released. Himple didn't have to hold on to send a message; he was already gripping on for all he was worth.

"My friends are in the cage and over the fire", he thought to Moira.

"No problem. I don't see well out here, but I will try!"

The dragon was still only half out. The snakelike Mboi Tata did have small wings with claws on. When Moira stretched out her wings, she messaged Himple to climb on. Himple climbed along the wing like a log with his leg on either side. When he got towards the end, Moira put him against the cage. Pod and Flora were not sure if to get out or not when Himple reached to unbolt the door. "Are sure it's safe, young dwarf?" asked Pod. "Trust me!" said Himple with an outstretched hand.

With Pod and Flora climbing up Moira to safety, Himple was moved closer to the fire. "Daddy! Daddy!" cried Flora from the safe position between Barnaby and Pod high on Moira's neck.

Grimtrunk, it had to be said, was quite a sight, stripped to his longjohns and looking rather red. Moira put her claws under the pole and flipped it away from the flames. He landed face down in a muddy pool, but the ropes snapped on impact. Much to the entertainment of the other dwarfs, he then proceeded to roll around like a happy pig covering himself in thick wet mud to cool his burns.

Himple even heard the thoughts of Moira as she chuckled at the sight of Master Grimtrunk covered in mud. As Himple looked around, the trolls were gathered in an area off towards the left of the mountain. Those that had not scarpered to the woods for their lives. Moira dropped her head for them to jump off and thought to Himple...

"Safe trip, my friend, Himple. I will keep them busy while you escape. I will always be grateful for your help. We are linked now in a special way. You have a truly special gift, Himple."

Himple held on for one last time. *"Thank you, Moira. I hope we meet again too."*

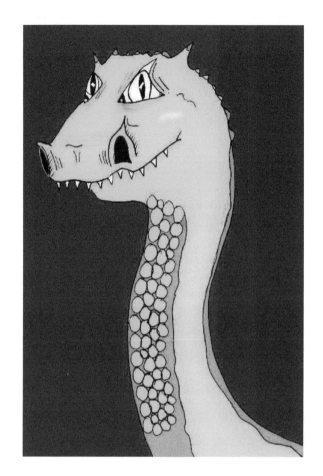

Moira

Chapter Thirteen: The Getaway

Pod passed Grimtrunk his axe and the clothes he had collected. "No time to change, let's get out of here!" said Himple. Flora climbed onto Pod and the dwarfs made for the trees. As the others entered the forest, Himple and Barnaby took one last look back. Moira was having a large meal, and trolls were on the menu.

They ran and ran until Pod shrieked with pain. They were an hour away, but he had hurt his ankle and fell to the floor, being sure to protect Flora as he did.

"Sorry all, I'm not as fit as I used to be," said Pod.

"It's okay. You're doing just fine", said a supportive and uncharacteristically friendly Grimtrunk. "Let's move off the path and take a break," said Himple, supporting Pod to get up as they moved forward to the edge of a clearing.

"Beware chupacabra!" Barnaby read from an old sign in the middle of the clearing. Everyone looked at Himple. He smiled in recognition of their trust in his knowledge. Himple cleared his throat, "Well, I have always wanted to see one. They are very rare. They are not very nice, I'm afraid. Think bloodsucking lizards the size of a bear."

The group's heads dropped, "We'd be better off fighting the trolls!" said Grimtrunk.

"Hungry," said Flora. Grimtrunk looked in his bag to find food. By the time he found a lonesome biscuit, Flora was sitting on Pod's knee eating a piece of cake. The look of happiness on Pod's face watching the young girl tuck in was a picture. "Thank you," said Grimtrunk. "My pleasure, we seem to have hit it off this young lady and me. I never had young ones, would have loved to be a Grandad…" said Pod sadly. Flora put down her cake and hugged Pod, somehow sensing his sadness. "Looks like you are one now!" said Grimtrunk, "Welcome to the family."

A few miles ahead on the same trail…

"Grub, Burk, what are you playing at!" snapped Trock, the tall, imposing leader of the trolls. We need to build a fire, or we will be drained of blood by the morning. These chupacabras are dangerous at night, and the darkness is approaching. "Fetch this, do that, go there and lift this..." Burk grumbled to Grub. "Soonist we gets this done, soonist we gets our feets up!" said Grub.

It was not long before the trolls sat around the fire, with a goat cooking on a makeshift spit over it.

Himple spotted the smoke as it rose through the trees. It was only ten minute walk ahead of them. "What do we think is making a fire?" Himple asked the others. "Making fire is not easy. It could be trolls," said Grimtrunk. "Let's get as near as possible without being detected. The wildlife will stay clear of the fire. We will need to mask our scent and stay silent. No snoring, Pod!" said Himple.

They found a tree with low branches and dense foliage. They climbed up high into the branches, and they could see the camp and trolls from their position. The trolls laid against tree trunks warming their feet by the fire, and their goat cooked. "Apple! Apple!" said Flora pointing at a strange fruit that hung down from the tree. "I think they are cashew fruit, am I correct, Pod?" asked Himple, pulling one from the tree. "I believe you are correct," said Pod, "The fruit is nice if it's ripe and it seems just right. Discard the nut that hangs from the bottom and munch away", he continued.

They all tucked in. There was plenty for all and with a full belly came a chance to relax and listen to the nighttime sounds of the forest. There were howls from the chupacabra, who feasted on the goats and wild boar that lived in the forest. They watched as the trolls ate their supper and set fire to burn till dawn, then they slept. Considering the strange environment, they slept rather well. Their sleep was, however, interrupted suddenly with a shaking of the tree.

"They's apples, I tells ya Burk, fill ya bag with um!" said Grub shaking the tree. The dwarfs were awake and holding tight to a tree branch. Well, all the dwarfs except for Pod, who was still fast asleep. The tree shook again, and Pod fell all the way down to the feet of the trolls. Pod hunted around for his glasses and looked up at a troll, thinking he was at home with his wife. "Good morning dear, I had the strangest dream. I was up a tree, is the kettle on?"

"I'll put you in my kettle!" said Grub. Pod realised where he was and what was in front of him. It was too late to grab his axe or run for cover. Burk had him.

So Pod was a large dwarf but was not much more than waist high on Burk. Burk tucked Pod neatly under his arm and squeezed. "Orrrhhh!" exclaimed Pod in pain. Then Trock appeared, "Burk, please don't squeeze all the juice out of whatever you have under your arm", he said in his sinister and devious manner.

Trock looked up to the tree and spoke again, "Now that we have our meal sorted, we can get back to the camp and persuade the king to send reinforcements to deal with that dragon. Tie him up and follow me." Himple held back

Barnaby, who seemed all for grabbing his axe and attacking the trolls. Once the trolls were out of sight, Grimtrunk spoke first, "Blithering Beards, whatever next! We were no match for those three. We need to follow and get him back." "I agree," said Himple, packing together his and Pod's leftover things. "Barnaby, are you okay?" Himple continued. Barnaby was clearly still very upset. He seemed dazed, breaking his silence to say, "When is this all going to end? When will we be home?"

Grimtrunk jumped to the ground with Flora in his arms, "Come on, soldiers! Axes ready for battle! You know I picked you two, I know I said I didn't. I regret saying it now, you have both really impressed me!" he said. Barnaby and Himple smiled at each other, and they followed the scent of the trolls along the track.

Chupacabra

Chapter Fourteen: Pod's Rescue

Fortunately, as you now know, trolls have a distinct odour, so the tracking was easy. The heavy brush of the forest made it easy to see the track they had taken. As they walked, each of the dwarfs wondered how they would rescue Pod. Whilst Grub and Burk were easy to deceive, their leader Trock was a very different proposition. They chatted quietly as they walked, coming up with ideas. Grimtrunk was keen on a surprise attack. Barnaby wanted to get ahead and attack from the trees. Whilst Himple was certain the other two's ideas would be met with certain failure, he was unsure of how to secure his friend's freedom. The dwarfs had been walking for several hours, and the midday sun was breaking through the trees sending spears of light down from the canopy.

"They're stopping!!" said Himple looking ahead. The dwarfs could hear water, fast-moving water. Barnaby climbed to get a better view. When he returned to the ground, he reported, "There is a vast river ahead, too deep to cross even for the trolls. There is a single wooden raft, only just big enough for two trolls, I would say."

Himple knew they had to seize their chance. They needed a diversion. "We need to distract the trolls and grab the raft to make our escape down the river," Himple told the others. "On a raft!" said Grimtrunk, who quickly had to be reminded to keep his voice down. "If one of us runs to the other end of the shoreline and shouts out, the trolls will follow them, leading them away from the raft. We can get on the raft and enter the river as we pass, the dwarf who distracted them can jump in the water and swim to the raft, and we can escape downstream." Both Barnaby and Grimtrunk looked terrified. "Problem?" asked Himple.

Now you need to know that dwarfs are proud, brave creatures, quick to battle and very slow to admit weakness. So, the fear on their faces worried Himple.

Barnaby was first to talk, "I can't swim, and I hate boats." Both Himple and Barnaby looked at Grimtrunk, "I … can't swim either, and well, I'm about as close to water now as I have ever been…."

Himple looked puzzled. "Ok, I will be a distraction and swim to the raft. Do you two think you can grab Pod and get the raft downstream?" The two nervous-looking dwarfs agreed, and Himple passed them his bag but kept his axe just in case. Grimtrunk passed Flora to Barnaby and went to the tree line. Pod was already on the raft bound with ropes on the riverside. Trock was checking the raft for seaworthiness with the other two trolls fashioning oars from tree branches.

Himple appeared not far downriver, on some large rocks. He shouted to the trolls.

This was the only part of Himple's plan that worked. Only Burk and Grub ran towards Himple. Trock stayed where he was. Grimtrunk and Barnaby were not sure what to do. Should they attack Trock or run to Himple's aid? They decided to stick to the plan, and they headed for the raft. Grimtrunk confronted Trock while Barnaby untied Pod and placed Flora on the raft. All three dwarfs raised their axes and attacked Trock, who turned and ran towards the other trolls who were pursuing Himple. Grimtrunk pulled back Pod, who was in pursuit. "We have a plan, we need to get on the raft. Himple will swim out to us." Grimtrunk explained.

Further up the river, Himple stood his ground. He could see the others were not yet on the river and needed to give them time so the troll would not turn back and get them. Fortunately, Burk and Grub were not the speediest of trolls. In fact, quite the opposite. Trock, the thinner, taller and meaner troll, was almost ahead of them when they reached the rocks where Himple stood. Himple edged to the furthest point of the rock that overhung the fast-running river water.

Back at the raft, they were on the water and heading downstream. Barnaby and Grimtrunk were laid face down on the raft, eyes closed, holding on as tight as possible. Flora was sat on Grimtrunk's back, cheering with excitement as Pod used a tree branch in an attempt to steer the raft down the river.

Grub and Burk were climbing the rocks, so Himple put his axe on his back and prepared to jump into the water. He could see Pod and others heading towards him, so he jumped for it. Himple had closed his eyes when he launched himself off the rocks, so he was shocked after a few seconds when he was not wet…

"GOT YOU!!" said Trock, grabbing Himple' leg. "You aren't getting away that easily!" Trock cackled like a witch as he carried Himple upside down by his leg on the riverbank where Burk and Grub were waiting.

Pod and the others looked on as the current swept them downstream and away, helpless to rescue Himple.

Trock

Chapter Fifteen: The Black Beast

There was a fierce fire in minutes, and the trolls made ready for a meal. Himple feared he was going to be on the menu. The two large trolls were looking for branches to make a spit over the fire. Trock stoked the fire and prodded Himple with his dagger. "Not much meat on them bones of yours. Still young flesh, you will make good sweet eating," he said. All of a sudden, Burk and Grub ran from the woods where they were collecting firewood. "What's wrong with you fools?!" asked Trock in a vicious voice. Grub replied, "There tis summut nasty in them woods, growlin and nasty." "Nastier than you two? What was it, a chupacabra? They feed on goat's blood; they wouldn't attack you!" said Trock in a condescending voice. Trock quite obviously thought himself above any ordinary troll.

Just then, there was a howl. A chupacabra for sure, and a deafening squeal. Then flying through the air from out of the woods came a large scaly creature, the size of a bear. It was dead.

"What tis it?" said Burk hiding behind the fire. "It's a very large and very dangerous chupacabra!" said Trock in a very concerned voice. "But don't worry about that. Worry about what killed it and threw it here," said Trock holding up his dagger and looking very afraid.

Then came the growl. It was terrifying! The trolls looked at each other. Then the growl came again. "You two go and see what it is. Arm yourselves!" said Trock, who pushed the two trolls towards the woods. Trock grabbed Himple and held him between himself and the woods. Himple thought he meant to throw him to whatever was out there and escape if it should come for him.

Burk and Grub approached the treeline slowly when a massive black and white creature jumped from the trees. It leapt over Burk and Grub and headed to Trock and Himple. As it flew toward Trock, it was clear it had two massive front teeth. Himple closed his eyes. Trock did not get a chance to throw Himple in its way. It was on Trock in an instant, biting clean off the arm that held Himple, and in turn, sending Trock backwards into the river and away in the current.

Himple looked up from the floor. He was still bound with rope but risked one look at the creature before what he thought was his certain death. Then the creature licked him and nuzzled him up into its giant arms.

Himple knew in an instant it was Mabel. "Girl! How did you get here?" Mabel licked him again and again before biting through the ropes that bound him. "I missed you too, girl. I missed you too."

Himple couldn't understand how he had been reunited with his pet buggane. How had she found him and rescued him? Himple was overjoyed it had happened, and that was all that matters. Himple remembered the other trolls and stood up and looked, but they were long gone.

"Mabel, we have to save my friends and get them home safe," said Himple, in the hope the buggane understood. Himple looked downriver for any signs, but before his mind had a chance to formulate a plan, Mabel had tossed him on her back and headed down the riverbank. The buggane, although said to be panda and mole in origin, was gorilla-like in posture and movement, bounding along in a crouched ape-like position. Himple held on to Mabel's back, holding fur but trying not to pull it. Mabel was quick to cover the ground. Himple had always longed for this moment, experiencing freedom with Mabel, if only it had been in less of a dangerous situation.

They saw Trock ahead. He was out of the water and was heading downstream on the other side of the river. Not much further ahead, there was a small inlet with a large sandy bank. There on the bank were his friends, with Trock heading in their direction.

Himple jumped down and started to the water. Mabel did not move. "Come on, girl!" Himple said, splashing the water with his hand. "It is not far across…" Himple said in his most reassuring voice. It was quite obvious Himple could add: afraid of water to his knowledge of bugganes. Himple waved and shouted across the river to Barnaby and the others. By the time he turned back to Mabel, there was just a hole in the ground with dirt shooting out like water from a hose.

On the other side of the river, Grimtrunk was panicking. "What sort of new horror is attacking Himple now? It's massive, and I can see its claws from here." Barnaby reassured him, "It looks like one of Himple's pets from home. He and his father keep them." Grimtrunk was still not sure, "Is it hiding?" he said, watching Mabel disappear underground.

They gathered their things and secured the raft. "We may need a volunteer to cross the river and rescue Himple. Or maybe we should be on that side of the river anyway?" They continued to argue and debate what side of the river they needed to be on to get back to the Realm Gateway.

"Got you! You didn't think I would give up on eating you so quickly, did you!" said Trock as he appeared from the bushes with a dagger in hand. Well, he only had one now. What was left of his other arm was bound with a sackcloth. Grimtrunk pushed Flora behind him. The dwarfs were on one side of the sandy inlet and Trock on the other. Grimtrunk looked across the river, but Himple had gone. Trock raised his dagger, "I will enjoy every last bit of you lot, roasted maybe," and he let out sinister laughs. He edged closer to Grimtrunk, step by step. When he was halfway across, there was a noise. A rumble from below, and then Trock stopped and sank a little into the sand.

Grimtrunk and the others watched as Trock sank deeper in, and then in an explosion of sand, Trock flew back towards the bushes as Mabel broke out of the ground like a jack-in-the-box. With Himple on Mabel's back, they landed between Trock and the others. Trock grabbed the stump where his arm was. Seeing Mabel brought back the pain of when she ate his arm.

"Are you okay?" asked Grimtrunk in astonishment at his student riding this truly monstrous creature. "Yes, meet Mabel. She is a pet and proving rather useful with trolls," said Himple.

"Unbelievable, I have never seen one up close in all my days!" said Pod. "I have seen them rip through bedrock like its bread," he continued.

They had quite forgotten that the evil Trock was right in front of them. Mabel hadn't. Her gaze was fixed on him.

Trock tried to seize his chance and lunged at Mabel with his dagger.

Before Trock could fully outstretch his arm, his hand with a dagger still gripped in his fingers fell to the floor. Mabel had bitten off his other arm at the elbow. Trock turned and ran.

"Grab him!" shouted Grimtrunk. "No, he is harmless now," said Himple. "You mean armless!" said Pod. They all laughed.

Himple and Mabel

Chapter Sixteen: Where Are We?

Barnaby collected wood, and the others looked for berries and roots to eat. Pod was quick to select some leaves that had been growing on the riverbank. As the others hustled and bustled at their tasks, Himple tended to Mabel. For the first time that day, he spent some time on Mabel and got her water from the river. Mabel hated the river and didn't want to go close...

As the others made camp for another night in this realm, Himple's thoughts wandered to home and how much his mum and dad would be worried. How Mabel had escaped and found the correct gate was too much of a coincidence. Horace Gwim was a very resourceful dwarf, and Himple hoped he would get a chance to thank him.

With the fire burning and their supper eaten, Himple laid with Mabel as his pillow. Flora had hidden from Mabel all evening but could no longer resist. She crept past Grimtrunk, her dad, and next to Himple, cuddling and stroking Mabel. Himple heard her say, "Good teddy, keep us safe."

They were up early and on track to follow the river away from the mountain. Grimtrunk and the others had agreed on a plan:

1. Follow the river until the mountain is as far away as when Barnaby first spotted it when they first arrived.
2. Circle the mountain, keeping it the same distance away until we find the familiar ground and the gateway.

They travelled along the bank for ages. Grimtrunk and Pod passed Flora between them as they walked, but the terrain was hard and rocky. Mabel made easy work of it, following Himple's every move. Himple spotted a tall tree ahead that looked like an easy climb. Barnaby was quick to scale it; he shouted to Himple, who climbed up too. When Himple got to where Barnaby had sat looking at the view, he realised Mabel was still in tow. The group giggled to see the tree bend with Barnaby, Himple and a very large Mabel sitting on a branch.

It was worth the climb. The view was spectacular. They were indeed very close to being the correct distance away from the mountain, and they could see various landmarks, but none looked familiar. To the right of the mountain was a clearer area with fewer trees. This was less likely to be the correct direction as they had spent most of their time above ground in the forest. However, there were clear signs of campfires to the left, with wispy threads of smoke coming from trees in a few areas. Whilst they had Mabel's protection, avoiding another encounter with trolls or worse would be their first choice.

Himple explained the options to Grimtrunk and Pod. "We need to go left for sure but need to spread out. We don't want to walk past the gate," said Grimtrunk. "That's true! I hadn't thought of that. What groups should we split into?" asked Himple. "You and the creature go slightly ahead, and we will follow by taking a wider route," Grimtrunk suggested. "Would you like Flora to ride on Mabel?" asked Himple. Grimtrunk thought hard. *"Put my child on the back of one of the most ferocious creatures in the dwarf world?"* He had never seen anything like Mabel but couldn't help agreeing she would be well protected. "Okay," agreed Grimtrunk.

Himple lifted Flora up onto Mabel, "Teddy Bear!" Flora said as she held on to the ripples of thick, soft black and white fur. Himple smiled at Mabel, living up to his expectations and more.

They set out the other dwarfs with axes in hand. Himple and Mabel made good ground, darting around on rocks and fallen trees. "Are you okay, Flora?" ask Himple. Flora simply replied, "Go Horsey! Faster, faster!!" Himple laughed and returned to scouting for the gate to send them home.

Behind them, Pod was struggling to keep up, mainly as he had to stop to take interesting seeds and cuttings from impressive plants and trees. "Guabiroba! Well, I'm blessed," said Pod reaching for his bag to get a cutting off the rare berry-producing plant. As Pod rummaged in amongst the green stems, he saw a larger scalier stem, the size of a log. Pod stopped in his tracks and stood absolutely still. The dwarfs had been calling out to each other from time to time. There was no reply from Pod for a while. This was first because he was busy foraging, and now because, well he was standing, rooted to the spot trying to be quiet. Barnaby was worried, "Pod. You okay?" *"Don't come. Don't come,"* thought Pod, slowly trying to retreat and reach for his axe at the same time.

"There you are, what's up, cat got your tongue?!" said Barnaby in a loud voice approaching Pod. Pod broke his silence "RUUUUUNNNN!" he shouted, grabbing his axe and tumbling backwards. Barnaby wanted to do as he was told, but his instincts said *grab your axe*.

From out of the bushes came a chupacabra, green and scaly and very well camouflaged in the forest. Its lizard-like face was blood-stained from its latest feed and hissed as it eyed up the fumbling Pod trying to get to his feet. Barnaby ran to get between Pod and the creature raising his axe for combat. The creature leapt at Barnaby with its teeth exposed. Barnaby didn't get a chance to swing his axe before the creature was on him, biting through his leather arm guards and into the dwarf's forearm. The weight of the bear sized chupacabra sat heavily on Barnaby's chest as the creature let go of his arm and eyed up to finish Barnaby off.

Then there was a swish of an axe, and the head of the beast came clean off. There, behind the headless creature, was Pod with Betty, his trusted old axe in hand.

"Nasty looking things!" said Pod, wiping Betty. "Let's get that arm of yours looked at," Pod continued helping up Barnaby.

Barnaby was stunned to silence, his face emotionless. When he regained his composure, he began to speak, "It was going to..." "It was going to give you a nasty nibble, but, oh look, what an interesting orchid!" With no concern from the encounter or his heroics, Pod toddled off to look once again at the plant life, leaving Barnaby in admiration of the old warrior and groundsman. "Echinacea! This is the ticket. Put this on the bite, young Barnaby," said Pod passing Barnaby some most pleasant purply pink flowers. "Crush and squeeze them in your hand first," Pod continued. Himple and Flora on Mabel's back suddenly burst through the bushes. Within seconds, Pod had Betty in his hand, and Barnaby dived for cover.

"Sorry to surprise you. We wondered where you were," said Himple, his eyes noticing the headless body of the chupacabra on the path. "Been busy, I see. Any more around?" asked Himple, trying to shield Flora's eyes from the corpse. It was too late, he realised, as he rode off to check the vicinity as Flora said, "Where's the dead froggy gone?!"

Himple knew it was unusual for a pack animal such as the chupacabra to be alone. He soon found Grimtrunk and warned him about the attack. Grimtrunk went off to find the others whilst Himple continued his search. Mabel was sniffing and clearly onto a scent. Himple was worried. Mabel slowed to a halt and pricked up her ears. "Shhh," said Himple to Flora, putting his fingers to his lips.

It did not, unfortunately, work as only a few seconds later, at the top of her voice, everyone with earshot heard Flora shout, "More froggies!!!" It was too late to retreat. Himple grabbed Flora as Mabel growled a noise that would rival a T-rex. They jumped off Mabel and made for cover, and as they landed, Himple reached for his axe, and Mabel launched into action. Like a vampire at the blood bank, Mabel went into full attack mode, tossing the massive chupacabras around like kittens with balls of wool. Mabel swiped her massive claws and snapped her teeth at the attacking beasts. One by one, each of the lizard-like bloodsuckers fell. Himple stood ready and watched over Flora. It was quite unlikely, however, that Mabel would allow anyone or anything to harm Himple. When Mabel was finished and had had a particularly large frog-leg lunch, Himple and Flora mounted up and went to find the others.

They reached the others, "Is everything okay? We heard growling?" said Grimtrunk. Himple replied, "Yes, everything's fine." "Teddy ate froggies!" said Flora. Everyone laughed.

Mabel, Himple and Barnaby

Chapter Seventeen: Where Is the Gate?

In the heat of the afternoon sun, the group began the search for the realm gate that had brought them on this adventure. Barnaby climbed trees to look for clues to get them home. Having encountered the creatures earlier, they were staying together now, and Mabel and Himple went first, checking the way. With the dense forest and undergrowth, the going was slow. Barnaby and Grimtrunk used their axes, and Pod followed behind with Betty in hand.

Back at the academy...

On his third attempt, General Groanbottom managed to get to his feet on the stage of the assembly hall. Parents and the students were gathered for a long-awaited update. Unfortunately, the chair had not stayed on the floor and was still attached to his rather large bottom. "What's going on? Guards! Guards! Get the blasted thing off my bottom!!!" shouted Groanbottom, who was by now very red in the face. In fact, if steam really did come out of ears, like in cartoons, it would have filled the room.

Groanbottom composed himself after two guardsmen managed with difficulty to remove the chair and then returned to the position in line on the stage. "Tomorrow morning at zero eight hundred hours, a crack team of mountain guards will leave this realm in a rescue mission. I am sure you will all be delighted to hear I will personally be leading the mission on the direct orders of the Brigadier himself," Groanbottom paused. There was an anonymous shout from the onlooker, "Do you even fit through the gate?" Groanbottom was not impressed, "Who said that? Well, I'll tell you! I have…" Once again, I will not bore you with the details but give you a synopsis of the 45 minutes of Groanbottom's remaining speech.

Groanbottom's great.

Groanbottom's killed stuff.

Groanbottom's great.

Groanbottom's killed stuff.

…Pork Pie Break…

Groanbottom's great.

Groanbottom's got a promotion.

Groanbottom's great.

That about sums it up…. until the Headmaster interrupted.

"This is absolutely fascinating, but I am sure the General has a lot of planning to do for tomorrow. Do we have any questions?"

Horace Gwim stood forward and spoke, "I would like to volunteer to go on the mission. I am an accomplished animal expert, and I know each of the missing dwarfs."

Well, the Headmaster looked across to the General, who was tucking into a particularly large pork pie. It had been brought out to him by the school chef. The chef was asking Groanbottom if he would like another delicious huge pork pie, and in uncontrollable excitement, he jumped to his feet and shouted, "FANTASTIC!"

"Well, that's good. Then it's settled. Mr Gwim will accompany the mission to rescue the missing team tomorrow!" said the Headmaster.

"What!" spluttered the General, but it was too late. It was agreed, and with a huff, Groanbottom sat back down and continued with his pork pie.

Back in the undergrowth…

Himple and Flora were waiting for the others in a clearing and sat snug on Mabel's back. The others soon arrived, and there was a despondent feeling in the group who seemed lost. Then hope came from a most unsuspected source. Flora gestured to Grimtrunk to come down from Mabel. Once on the floor, she ran to a bush and picked some pretty yellow flowers. She put some in her hair. Then Himple remembered, "The yellow flowers are the same ones we saw when we arrived. They were the clue that set us on our trail." Himple had excitement in his voice. Pod was over in a flash and examined the flower, confirming, "He is right. This is the same flower."

They knew they were close, but by now, the sun was setting. Barnaby climbed a tree once more to look for clues as to their best way forward.

"Smoke up ahead!" Barnaby called down. Himple climbed up beside Barnaby to get a good look. Himple could see multiple spirals of smoke; there was definitely some kind of encampment. It looked like a good hour's walk from their position, and the sun was getting lower on the horizon. "We need to check out the camp without being caught," said Grimtrunk. The dwarfs all looked at each other. Dwarfs were many things, but quiet and stealth-like was definitely not one of them.

"The creature is too conspicuous. Barnaby and I are hard to hide. Pod, my old friend, I hope you don't mind me saying you are prone to a clumsy fall or two." Grimtrunk continued.

"That leaves me," said Himple, deep in thought. "If I go, I'm not sure Mabel will stay here, and as you say, she would be hard to hide. Let's give it a go," Himple said, gathering his bags and axe.

Himple went over to Mabel and stroked her. He told her she needed to stay with the others and he would be back soon. Mabel looked up at Himple, and he could see the concern in her eyes. They agreed to hide out near the yellow flowers, and Grimtrunk told Himple he had two hours to return or Grimtrunk would come for him. "Should we tie Mabel up?" Grimtrunk asked. "I'd like to see you try!" laughed Himple, and he made way to the edge of the clearing.

Mabel stood to follow Grimtrunk. Pod and Barnaby moved quickly out of her way as she started to move, only for Mabel to be confronted by Flora. "Teddy, STAY!" she said in her biggest voice and to everyone's astonishment, Mabel did. "She has her Guides Animal Training Badge, from her Rainbows Dwarf Pack ... I'm very proud," said Grimtrunk with a mixture of fear and admiration for his daughter.

General Groanbottom

110

Chapter Eighteen: Not Again!

Himple moved quickly on his own, taking an odd look back to check Mabel was not following him. The smell gave it way before there was any chance to get a good view of the encampment. Troll's again. Himple climbed a tree once he got as close as he dared. It was high, and by the time he got to the top, he had a full view, twice the number of trolls he had seen at the mountain, all of them in small groups around a fire.

There, in the centre, was the Realm Gate, were two familiar trolls from back at the river and another troll who looked massive and wore a crown. *"He must be the King,"* Himple thought. He sat on a chair made from tree trunks. Himple could see Burk and Grub talking to King troll, explaining what had happened with the dragon and Mabel, Himple surmised.

Himple carefully descended the tree and made his way back to the camp. As he weaved his way through the undergrowth, he had a feeling of despair at the thought of having to get past more trolls. There was little hiding going on when he returned to the clearing with the yellow flowers. Grimtrunk, Barnaby and Pod were sitting nervously on a log, watching Mabel. At first, all Himple could see was Flora's back, with most of Mabel's head obscured. Then seeing

Himple, she turned around, saying, "Teddy looks pretty!" Flora moved to reveal Mabel (the savage beast, untrainable buggane) with a headdress of yellow flowers and flowers behind her ears. "Unbelievable! Good girl, Mabel!" said Himple and turned to others. Grimtrunk stood with a look of relief that Himple had returned. Mabel instantly growled, and Grimtrunk sat back down and spoke, "I think when you said stay, Mabel is enforcing the situation for all of us. I can't believe her intelligence. It is remarkable. What did you find out?"

Himple relayed his discovery and the two trolls talking to the crowned troll. Pod explained the Troll King was often the largest and most ferocious troll winning the crown through killing the previous king rather than inheriting the title. Himple said the troll numbers were in the hundreds, and the gate was well guarded.

There was a period of silence, and Himple spoke, "I think we need a distraction to lead some of the trolls away to give us enough time to get through the gate and home." Grimtrunk agreed, saying, "It might have to be more than one diversion with this many trolls." The dwarfs planned long into the night as Flora fell asleep on Mabel after a meagre meal of leaves and berries prepared by Pod. Grimtrunk's eyes kept looking toward his daughter. "She is okay, you know. Mabel won't hurt her," said Himple, noticing his gaze.

Behind the very large clearing with the Realm Gate was an embankment of gravel and a stone face leading up to the higher ground. Himple had spotted this and had not seen any trolls up there overlooking the encampment. Once up and ready, this was their first port of call. They crept through the undergrowth and up a hill that led to the good viewpoint.

Quite remarkably, the area overlooking the camp was troll-free. They were level with the treetop and had the perfect view. Mabel and Flora stayed well back, and the four dwarfs on hand and knee crawled to the edge of the viewpoint to see below.

They watched the coming and goings, mainly trolls, bring the King food and drink. Then there was a faint hum, a familiar hum. "The gateway has been activated," said Himple. The others heard it too, and unfortunately, so did the trolls who followed a roar of instruction from the King, and they rallied to the gate with spears and swords in hand.

Six mountain guards appeared one after another, each grabbed and disarmed by the trolls. The last one was a particularly large guard who made a lot of noise. Then one further person. Himple didn't recognise him at first. Then snapped, "Dad!" before quickly backing away to check he hadn't been spotted. It was okay. The trolls were too busy with their catch. Grimtrunk looked furious, "Not only do we need to escape, but we need to rescue them now too!!" He was not happy. The trolls held their captives at the opposite end of the camp to the gateway so as not to give them a chance to make a break to the gateway for freedom.

Himple spoke to his friends, "The plan hasn't changed. We still need a diversion; we just need to free the captives too. It is obvious Mabel will make for a good diversion, but we need to make the trolls leave the far side of the camp as well as the gateway." They all thought. Pod suggested escape and sending back help for the others until Grimtrunk pointed out the rescuers would wait days before coming.

Himple spoke again, a plan formulating in his mind. "The gateway will need dialling back to the academy. We could send Flora through to safety with a message and then try to help the others. With Mabel by the gate, she will have safe passage, and it will send the trolls towards the captives." "Then what?" said Pod, "Mabel is scary, but there are an awful lot of trolls up that side of the camp."

Barnaby was not one generally for good ideas, but the confidence of being with friends gave him the belief to speak. He stuttered, to begin with, but found his voice, "Fire!

They didn't like the fire. Even when the dragon had moved on, they hated the fires left behind. There is a pile of logs further along this ridge. Look over there. Could we set fire to them and push them down?" "It would be easier if we had a dragon, but that's not a bad idea, Barnaby," said Grimtrunk. Barnaby grinned from ear to ear with the praise from his axe master.

The group were waiting for Himple to pass comment on the plan, but he was deep in thought. Then he finally spoke, "the gateway stones work using ancient psychic energy, that's what we are told. The energy dates back to when time began. I read that if you communicate telepathically with a powerful creature, the residue of that energy stays with you for some time after. If I can touch the gateway, I may be able to get a message to Moira." "If Barnaby and I could set the logs on fire, would that give you enough time to get to the gateway, dial-up and send Flora through, then you could try to communicate to the dragon?" Grimtrunk excitedly asked, pleased about the plan taking shape. "I don't know," admitted Himple, "But it's worth a try!"

So it was set. Pod would go to the Gate with Himple, Mabel and Flora, and the other two would make the diversion.

There was quite a commotion going on with General Groanbottom trying to lecture the Troll King about his rights as a captive. "I will have you know I have been captured by scarier creatures than you! And worse smelling ones!! And that says something! May I remind you that as a captive, I have the right to trial? I have the right to basic rations." Groanbottom was in full flow when the King interrupted him, "You have the right to be stewed in a pot and eaten, but I am concerned you will be a bit too fatty!"

Horace Gwim tried to get a word in. "We could trade you something for our release? Something VALUABLE!" I think the only word the King heard was valuable, but it did get his attention. "What kind of valuables?" the King asked.

Horace had not got a plan or anything valuable to offer, so he was clearly now in trouble. "Secrets!" came blurting out of Horace's mouth. It was clear he had not considered the type of secrets; however, it was enough to get the King thinking.

High over them, Barnaby and Grimtrunk were working on the pile of logs, setting them alight. They were very dry, so the task was an easy one. They looked across from their position and saw the others were ready for their part of the plan. They pushed the logs (there must have been 30) down off the ridge and the gravel embankment and into position between the trolls and the gateway. It wasn't completely successful; there was a group of trolls, maybe eight still on the gateway side, but for now, their attention was on fire.

Himple and Flora, on Mabel's back, jumped down to the gateway in what had to be two impressive leaps. With Betty in hand, Pod gave pursuit. Tripping over a large stone, he fell forward, tumbling head over heels as he fell down the ridge and all along the embankment. Pod finally stopped rolling as he hit the vine-covered gateway. He stood to attention, saluted and then fainted. Himple ignored Pod and went straight to work, dialling the gateway home for Flora.

The trolls were running around panicking as the King barked orders. The logs had formed a fence of fire, and the King had sent a burly group of trolls in the direction of where the logs came from. The trolls were only too pleased to get away from the fire. Grimtrunk and Barnaby were now in danger, so they headed to the others.

The sound of the gate activating was heard even over the panic, and the trolls on the gateway side of the fire turned and headed towards Himple's position.

It was too late. The gate had been activated, and Flora was through before they got close. Mabel moved swiftly into position between Himple, his owner and the oncoming trolls.

117

Himple turned his attention to Pod, who had by this time sat up with his helmet over his eyes. He shouted in a confused voice, "Hello, Hello! Is there anybody there? I think I'm in a dark cave? Himple? Master Grimtrunk? Anyone?"

Himple lifted Pod's helmet to give him some daylight. He stood up with a start and grabbed his axe, Betty. The trolls, well, most of them, had spotted Mabel and had stopped. They were scratching their heads, wondering what it was in front of them. One troll, however, was unaware his fellow attackers had stopped and continued his charge to the gateway and the awaiting Mabel. (I have been warned against being too graphic in my text on the fight scenes but let's just say, within two seconds of the trolls attack on Mabel, the poor troll had no need for a hat and nothing to put on his shoulders anymore.)

With the troll body lying on the floor, Mabel looked slowly up at the other trolls. Now, as I have explained, trolls were terrified of fire, but Himple could now add to his study that they were more scared of Mabel!! The trolls ran headlong through the fire to the other side and safety from Mabel.

Grimtrunk and Barnaby joined the group, and Grimtrunk hugged Himple, "Thank you and well done!" Himple was shocked. What a long way he had come with his axe master in such a short time.

As the fires from the logs continued to roar, Himple once again went to the gateway. He touched it. Then he hugged it. Then he pushed his head against the stone, and he thought as he had done in the cave with Moira.

"Moira, Help Us!" Himple repeated again and again.

"How will she know where we are?" asked Grimtrunk. "Can she follow your signal?" Grimtrunk continued. Himple let the gateway go, "I don't know. Sorry, I'm pretty new to telepathy. I hope she can see the smoke!"

All of a sudden, the somewhat dazed Pod started rummaging in his bag. "Mountain Guards always carry a flare in case they get separated from the group in the mountains. I was given this one… Well, I'm not sure how many years; I'm 200 next birthday." Pod, with flare in hand, set about sending the red tower of smoke shooting into the air. There was a sense of satisfaction on Pods face as he did it.

"The fire is dying down!" said Barnaby, who was on the lookout. Even Mabel looked up from finishing off some particularly green trolls legs.

They moved in sight of the captured dwarfs where the Troll King was still barking orders. As they watched, there was the sound of falling gravel from the ridge. There were maybe 50 trolls above them on the ridge, looking down and shouting. The dwarfs grouped together, axes in hand. Mabel joined them. The fires were receding, and there were gangs of trolls waiting to pounce once the fire allowed. The King troll was shouting up to the trolls on the ridge, telling them to attack. The trolls could clearly see Mabel from their position and were staying put.

On the other side of the fire, Horace, Groanbottom and the others were still tied up, "If you let us free, we will put out the fire for you," Horace suggested. The King looked at him; he knew something was happening near the gateway but wasn't sure what. He knew there was something over there that the trolls on the ridge were not happy about.

"Let them all go, but this one stays with me!" The King said, pointing at Groanbottom. "If you deceive me, he is next on the fire!" the King proclaimed. As the dwarfs were released, Groanbottom was recounting a story of him battling the great mountain fires of years gone by. To hear him speak, he put the whole forest fire out on his own, with just a floppy beater and flask of tea.

When Horace got to the fire, he could clearly see the dark outline of Mabel and the other dwarfs, and his heart lifted. The flames were still quite high, but he and the soldier used their axes to break down the logs. The King with Groanbottom tied up in front of him headed for the ridge, leaving just a few guards watching the soldiers and Horace closely.

When the King reached the summit, he could see what was worrying the others. "What is it?!" he asked. There was no reply. One pointed out the remains on the floor next to Mabel. "You, you and you!" The King said, pointing at the largest of his subjects on the ridge and then continuing. "Take spears and approach the beast. Take this annoying dwarf with you and if you are attacked, feed him to the creature. Maybe it is scared of fire? Take a torch each too!" With torches raised and the rest of the trolls edging down the ridge behind them, the fire did work. It had Mabel spooked. Himple comforted her, "It's all right, girl."

As the trolls took up a position at the bottom of the ridge, there was a break in the main fire from the logs, and Horace ran towards his son, followed by the other soldiers. Horace could see Mabel and, in normal circumstances, would not approach her, but these were not normal times. He ran to his son and hugged him. Mabel growled and nudged Horace away from Himple and then gave him a big lick. This terrified Horace more than the trolls. The soldiers behind joined the knot of dwarfs (that's what you call a group of dwarfs, although some say it should be curmudgeon like badgers.)

The Troll King

Chapter Nineteen: Final Face-Off

So it had come to this, Grimtrunk looked on at the trolls, now all with torches as the King had seen the effect on Mabel. There were hundreds of them, the width of their pack the size of a football pitch.

The soldiers spoke to Grimtrunk, telling him they should leave when they had a chance, despite their General being held captive. Horace spoke up, "Leave him here. Let's go when we have a chance." The trolls were edging forward, trying to force them away from the relic Temple Gateway. Considering these were mountain guards, they were very keen to abandon Groanbottom and escape. Grimtrunk went to the front and addressed the dwarfs, "You may be mountain guards, but there is only one true leader on this mission; he has saved us all and shown bravery far beyond his years. I have learnt the hard way over the last few days to value those in my team. Himple, what's our next move?" There was a nod of approval and regret from Grimtrunk to Horace; the look said more than any apology ever could have.

"Well said, Master Grimtrunk," said Horace. Himple reluctantly stepped forward and spoke, "We save everyone. If we leave now, we only put more dwarfs at risk when they send another rescue mission. Let's try to get the General back."

Himple stepped forward with Mabel at his side and shouted to the King, "We will leave and never return if you release our fellow dwarf."

The Troll King laughed and poked Groanbottom hard with his spear. He replied, "I am not missing out on a meal out of this dwarf. Have you seen how much meat is on him?" The trolls widened their group and tried to surround the dwarfs. Whilst the trolls didn't like fire, they were passing fire-lit torches to one another, knowing that Mabel was retreating from them. The King moved forward; he was still some way away from the gateway and Himple.

"What do you want in exchange for our General? We could make a trade!" shouted Himple. It was clear there was going to be a negotiation now. Pod moved alongside Himple with Betty, his axe, at his side.

Himple stood forward, "I trained this creature. If you let the General go, I will tell you my secret!" The trolls were creeping forward. Pod drew close to Himple, with Grimtrunk and his dad on his other shoulder, "There are too many to fight, young dwarf. We would make a good hole in them, but there are just too many!"

The King stepped forward even more, "I will get the secret one way or another!" There must have been one hundred lit torches in front of Himple. They were an absolutely terrifying sight. Groanbottom wriggled and protested. He even offered the king the extra-large pork pie in his backpack if he freed him.

"On my mark!" said the King, "Charge them and kill them all!" Himple grabbed his axe. "Last chance to run," said Horace.

There was silence. Himple could feel himself shaking. Barnaby pushed past the others. "They will have to get past me to get you Himple!" he said, raising his axe. Pod agreed, "Me too!" There was a growl, and Mabel, sensing the oncoming danger, leapt over the dwarfs and stood between them and trolls.

"We will overpower your pet. He can't kill us all!" said the King, and he raised his dagger and torch aloft. The King then shouted, "Charge!"

Then there was a great rumble, like an earthquake. At first, Himple thought all the trolls were stamping their feet, like some African tribal dance, but it was not that. The trolls were not stamping. In fact, they were not moving and, more importantly, not charging. One or two had dropped their

125

daggers. The King was motionless, like a statue, looking directly at them.

"What's going on?" asked Grimtrunk, resting his axe on the floor. "I'm not sure. They look paralysed," replied Himple. The silence was eerie. Then the dwarfs fell into shadow as if a black cloud was above them.

Himple looked up, and to his amazement, he recognised the scales overhead straight away. The dwarfs parted, and Moira rested her head next to Himple. She touched Mabel, and they communicated immediately as friends through their fondness for Himple.

Moira had sensed Mabel's dislike of the torches and blew out all of the torches that the trolls held aloft, like candles on a birthday cake. Himple jumped on Mabel's back and headed toward Groanbottom and the King, with his axe raised. The Troll King turned and fled, followed swiftly by all the other trolls, screaming as they ran, and started to scramble up the bank. Groanbottom looked up at Mabel and Moira and put his hand over his eyes, curling up into a ball, shaking. Himple jumped down from Mable and tapped the General on the shoulder.

"It's okay; we've rescued you. Let's get you home," said Himple, helping the General up. The soldiers joined them and supported their General.

Himple went up to Moira and touched her face.

"Thank you, my friend," thought Himple.

"You're welcome, Himple. You are very special."

Himple looked at his dad and said, "Telepathy is cool." His dad picked up courage and approached Moira and his son. Horace placed his hand on Moira, and nothing happened. "Can you hear her?" asked Himple. "No, nothing." Himple placed his hand on his father's.

"You have a special gift, Himple," thought Moira

With Himple's hand on Horace's, he could hear, "I heard, I heard!" he said.

Mabel put her paw onto Himple's and across Moira.

"You are so very special, Himple. You see the souls of creatures. You connect to us like no other. You are my friend," thought Mabel.

"Mabel, you can talk! You can talk! Thank you for protecting us," Himple thought and spoke aloud.

Grimtrunk put his hand on Himple's shoulder. "Time to go, dial us home!" he said.

"Goodbye Moira, I hope to see you again in the future," thought Himple.

Moira turned back towards the dwarfs and smiled, then followed the trolls.

Himple went to the gateway and dialled home.

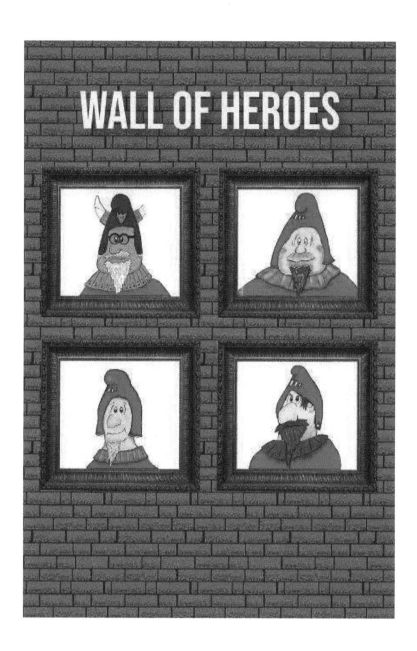

Chapter Twenty: A Hero's Return.

One week later at home with Himple…

"He is supposed to be dressed in his best uniform, and you have to leave in 10 minutes. Where is he? In that enclosure! It's your fault Horace Gwim, all your fault!" said Mrs Gwim.

Horace Gwim took the hint. He was in his best tunic and boots and walked out to the enclosure. Himple sat next to Mabel, enjoying the sun. "Time to go, son!" said Horace. Himple looked at his dad. "Mabel says she likes your boots," said Himple. "Tell her we will bring her back some treats from the feast!" said Horace. He had come to terms with the fact that Himple's telepathic connection to Mabel was still strong. In fact, in the week they had been back, Himple had shown communication skills with many creatures.

When they arrived at the academy later that morning, the whole place was buzzing. There were flags and decorations. Mountain guards hung around, chatting. First years were waiting to catch a glimpse of the heroes. In just a short week, the story of their adventure had been told in the papers, school hallways and taverns alike. Today was the official Feast of Valour, where heroes are celebrated for great acts of courage. There had not been one in Himple's memory. He was a little apprehensive and very honoured.

As guests of honour, Himple took his place on the stage. On the stage already were Barnaby, Pod and Grimtrunk. They hadn't seen each other much since they returned. Pod had returned to his duties in the gardens and grounds of the academy and had been planting the seeds and cultivating the cuttings he had taken whilst away. Grimtrunk had taken the brunt of the official stuff, telling the story of their adventure, making sure Groanbottom's useless contribution was not twisted to make him a hero.

The place was packed; there was no room for anyone else. Horace had a reserved seat on the front row with Grimtrunk's family, including Flora. There was a fanfare of trumpets, and three dwarfs walked to the centre of the stage, where there was a podium and three chairs. The Headmaster was followed by the General and then the Brigadier. Groanbottom looked completely miserable and sat down next to the Brigadier, allowing the Headmaster to take the podium.

The Headmaster began his address. "Welcome here today, one and all. The story of the rescue of Flora Grimtrunk will be told for generations to come, and we need to celebrate the heroes that made it possible. Master Grimtrunk showed great resolve and insight in taking a team that others would not have chosen. Groundsman and former mountain guardsman, Podwick proved he still had much to offer even at his age. Barnaby Grabbage proved that believing in yourself and looking after your team is a great strength. Lastly, Himple, who had gone about his academy life with little fuss and few accolades until now, but has proved to us all that knowledge is strength. I have a special announcement regarding the two students on the mission. They will both receive perfect marks and a full pass of their DRAGS end of year exams, allowing both to graduate with full honours."

Barnaby could not contain himself, and he jumped for joy, grabbing Grimtrunk in excitement. Himple let out a big sigh of relief. With that announcement over, the Headmaster took a seat, and the Brigadier took the podium and spoke, "Whilst I cannot condone the sending of missions with students and inexperienced travellers, I am without doubt as impressed with the story as all of you, and I hope these young heroes will consider a future in the military. The Medal of Honour will be given to each of the team members for not only saving Flora Grimtrunk but also rescuing the team sent to save them." The Brigadier gave the General a look of disgust.

Once the medals were presented and the feast began, the Headmaster came over to Himple, Barnaby and Pod and said as a special reward he had something very interesting to show them. He hoped the young dwarfs would consider further studies and maybe being masters in the future. They followed the Headmaster through the corridors of the academy to an area that was normally off-limits, leading them into an open cave. It was wet as a waterfall fell from the far side of the cavernous room. There was an underground stream that ran across the cavernous room, then down a steep slope of shiny rocks to small pools. "What do you think?" asked the Headmaster. He was expecting a WOW or similar. Barnaby and Pod looked at each other, a little confused. "It's a nice waterfall, Headmaster, very nice indeed," said Pod. The Headmaster was going to react, but Himple beat him to it. "It's a gateway! Carved around a cave entrance under the waterfall. It's concealed by the waterfall in front of it," said Himple, who was scrambling down to get a closer look. Barnaby followed instinctively.

The Headmaster explained, "This is the biggest secret of the academy, and you can tell no one about it. This is the mythical Gateway to Nowhere. Those who go through it have never returned. There is no control to dial up a destination. The ancient text of the academy says the destination is a mystery, one of time and travel". Himple and

Barnaby had reached the waterfall. They were looking through, trying to glimpse the destination...

"There are lights and shapes through the water. I can smell a flower," said Himple.

"Flowers? Maybe I can identify the scent. I'm coming down!" said Pod.

"Noooooo!" shouted Barnaby, "It's slippery!"

It was too late. Pod slipped, fell and took off!!! He flew through the air, off the slippery rocks and hit Himple and Barnaby, sending all three of them through the waterfall and into the Gate to Nowhere!.

The three dwarfs shook themselves and stood up.

Himple wiped his eyes as he could believe what he was seeing.

Himple panicked, his voice shaking, "Is that a dinosaur?!?!..."

The Gateway To Nowhere

Where has Himple gone, is a clue what you need?

The Gateway to Nowhere and another hero's deed.

Book Two is full of danger, a monster large and grumpy,

Help is needed once again, their new friend will be humpy

The Handcart holds a little clue, its name is the begining

Next comes the opposite of days, that's got your mind spinning

A place that lived Aladdin, and a lot more magic to boot

One thing for sure with Pod there it's going to be a hoot

A location of much intrigue, and much danger from the past,

Don't get the hump before Book Two your patience it must last!